JULIE
AND THE
PHANTOMS
The Edge of Great

Micol Ostow

Scholastic Inc.

ISBN 978-1-338-71337-4

10 9 8 7 6 5 4 3 2 1   21 22 23 24 25
Printed in the U.S.A.   40

First printing 2021

Book design by Jessica Meltzer

Background photos © Shutterstock.com

For Mazzy and Nonie,
     my favorite groupies.
               ~M. O.

Prologue

Luke

I'd totally love to tell you that, in the moment, I was focused on the unique vibe that sets in right before a show. Like the way the room is empty except for you and your bandmates, but also thrumming with energy. How the floors smell like a mix of sticky sweat and spilled drinks and ammonia that's not even making a dent in everything underneath.

I'd love to say that, but it's not true. Because right before a show—heck, *during* a show—anytime I'm playing music, really, the only thing I'm focused on is *me*.

Cocky? Okay, sure, if you insist. But it's the truth. When I'm playing, I go to a place inside myself that's separate from the whole outside world.

Don't get me wrong—I'd die for my bandmates. Alex, Reggie, and Bobby . . . the four of us, we're not just Sunset Curve, we're practically brothers. That's how it's always been. How it'll always be.

Of course—*as* Sunset Curve, we totally rock.

And tonight? Tonight was *our* night. We were finally here: The Orpheum. Los Angeles, California. Sunset Curve was about to become big-time. This was our break, the night that was going to change everything.

An amp buzzed, followed by the sound of Bobby plugging in his guitar.

Alex followed, counting us in with his drumsticks. *"One, two, three, four . . ."*

With the crash of a cymbal, I jumped in, wailing on my guitar. Chords flowed from my fingertips as they skated across the guitar strings. It was "Now or Never," our opening song, and we belted it out like we meant every last note—because we did.

All around us, a frenetic light show sliced glowing arcs against the walls, flashing with the crescendos of the music. The whole space felt totally cool and otherworldly.

Don't look down / 'Cause we're still
rising / Up right now

And even if we / Hit the ground /
We'll still fly / Keep dreaming

like we'll live forever / But live
it like it's now or never

It's now or never

I poured every piece of myself into that song, every last bit of my *soul*. And my boys did, too. I could hear it in the reverberation from their instruments, in the strong, soulful pitch to their voices as we all harmonized . . . but even more than hearing it, I *felt* it. In the air, in the space between the four of us, the energy that we created together.

When the song was over, from the VIP section, a lone club employee applauded. Dishcloth slung over one shoulder, she gave a few cheers and whoops as she clapped, definitely down with our music.

Reggie leaned into his microphone. His forehead was sweaty and he was breathing heavily, but his eyes were shining. "Thanks! We're Sunset Curve," he said, winking.

Okay, fine—showtime was two hours away. This was still just sound check. But Sunset Curve was *slammin'*. The waitress was beaming like we'd killed it, and our sound engineer was sending us a huge thumbs-up from his booth. "Great job, guys," he called.

"Too bad we wasted *that* on a sound check," Bobby joked, giving everyone a high five. "That's the tightest we ever played."

"'Til tonight," I corrected him, "when this place is packed with record execs."

For months now—maybe even years, if I'm honest—it felt like Sunset Curve had been hovering just on the edge of something huge. I know, I know . . . we were only seventeen. But we had serious *talent*. I knew it in my gut, in my bones . . . All we needed was our big break.

And it looked like our moment was finally here. *Tonight*. So close I could practically reach out and touch it. I just needed all the other guys to be *on* it, one hundred percent. Which meant totally positive attitudes. And from the way everyone was vibing right now, I knew we were good to go.

Reggie turned to Alex. "You were smokin', Alex," he said, nodding with appreciation.

Alex shrugged. I knew he appreciated the compliment and maybe even agreed—but unlike me, he was too humble to admit it out loud.

"Ah, I was just warming up," he protested. "*You* guys were the ones on fire."

Reggie gave him a mock glare. "Would you just own your own awesomeness for once?"

Alex blinked, slowly realizing that now the three of us were *all* staring at him, waiting.

He burst out laughing. "Okay," he admitted. "I was killin' it."

Alex jumped off his platform, and one by one, we moved off the stage. My stomach gave a rumble that reminded me it had been hours since we'd last eaten. We probably had just enough time to grab something before it was time to go on. I waved to the guys.

"Come on, we need fuel before the show. Let's get some dogs." Hot dogs were basically all we'd eaten since we'd started preparing for this gig—we weren't exactly rolling in cash. But I didn't mind. Soon we'd be big enough stars that we could eat in a different restaurant every night (if we didn't care about getting mobbed by fans, that is. Which I definitely did *not*).

We all grabbed our jackets and moved toward the door. All except Bobby. He was standing at the bar, watching as the waitress who'd clapped for us folded up her floral-print jacket and tucked it away for her shift. Next to her, by the register, was a pink flower in a vase that was so totally out of sync with everything else in the dingy club, I wondered if she'd put it there herself.

Reggie and Alex hovered at the front door, looking impatient. I glanced at Bobby. "You comin'?"

He waved me off. "I'm good." To the waitress he said, "Vegetarian. I could never hurt an animal."

I smirked. I'd heard that line before. And whether it was true or not (hint: it wasn't), Bobby wouldn't have mentioned it if he weren't trying to impress this girl. I could hardly blame him; she was *cute.* Maybe he was being slightly cheesy, but that was just the way Bobby got sometimes. We still had his back, same as we knew he had ours. *Bandmates for life,* we liked to say.

And this girl, she looked impressed, like his showing off was working. Like we were already as big as Weezer or Smashing Pumpkins or something. Ready to play the Orpheum as the main show and not just the opening act. Not just poised to take off but actually flying high.

"You guys are really good," she said. But she didn't say it just to Bobby. She said it to all of us, and it was clear from the look in her eyes how much she meant it.

"Thanks," I said, trying to be modest. (It was a new look for me, I'll admit. I'm not sure I nailed it.)

"No, really," she insisted. "I see a lot of bands. Been in a couple myself. I was feeling it."

So were we, I wanted to say. But she could tell that already, and besides, I had to play it cool. "That's what we do this for," I said, reaching a hand out to shake. (It wasn't like Bobby had dibs or anything, was it?) "I'm Luke."

The others chimed in. "I'm Reggie."

"Alex."

"Bobby."

"Nice to meet you guys," she said, smiling. "I'm Rose."

Reggie stepped closer to her, handing her a T-shirt and a CD. "Here's our demo and a T-shirt. Size"—he gave her a teasing glance—"beautiful."

Alex stepped forward to intercept the awkward cheese of the moment. "No, Reggie. Just, no." To Rose he said, "Sorry."

She just laughed, shrugging. "Thanks. I won't use this one to wipe down the tables."

Bobby cleared his throat. "Don't you guys have hot dogs to get?" he reminded us, shooting us a meaningful look. Maybe he hadn't called dibs, but he had a plan, and the rest of us were definitely in the way.

He looked so ticked, I couldn't resist giving it back to him a little. I leaned in toward Rose like I had a secret. Pointing at Bobby, I fake-whispered, "He had a burger for lunch."

Bobby's mouth snapped open, indignant, as Rose laughed. Reggie, Alex, and I grabbed our stuff, and we were off.

The side door of the Orpheum slammed shut behind us as we stepped into the dusk. Outside, the sounds of traffic—cars honking, people talking to each other as they made their way down the sidewalk—filled the air. Above us, the marquee showed *our* name: SUNSET CURVE. And beneath that, in letters just as big: SOLD OUT.

SOLD OUT. I let the words fill me up, like I was a helium balloon. As we rounded the corner of the block, I could see a line beginning to form for the club.

For *us.* That line was forming of people who couldn't wait to hear us perform. I threw my arms around Alex and Reggie, totally in the moment.

"That's what I'm talking about!" I said, that helium-balloon feeling bubbling up, out of control.

Alex pinched his face up. "The smell of Sunset Boulevard?"

I had to admit, at rush hour, there *was* a smell situation that was definitely not great. But even that—and another angry honk—couldn't get me down. Not now. "What that girl said in there," I explained, patient. "About our music. It's like an energy. It connects us with people. I want that connection with everyone." There was nothing like the feeling that came over me when I played my music for an audience.

Reggie paused for a minute, thinking it over. "We're gonna need more T-shirts."

"Three hot dogs, please." I didn't really even need to place the order—we were regulars here.

Sam 'N' Ella's Dogs was definitely *not* on the list of Hollywood hot spots for fine dining; the hot dog cart actually gave greasy spoons a bad name. But I wasn't going to complain since this place was keeping us going. Starving to death before we'd even had a chance to play the Orpheum—could you imagine anything lamer? At least James Dean went in a blaze of glory, right?

Sam handed us our dogs and I went to grab the ketchup. Which—along with the mustard, sauerkraut, and the rest of the toppings—were all served out of Sam's trunk. Maybe it was quaint. At the very least, one day we'd look back on this time in our lives and laugh . . .

Or so I hoped.

"I can't wait to eat someplace where the condiments aren't served out of the back of an Oldsmobile," Alex said, echoing my thoughts. He turned to the vendor. "Sorry, I got some pickle juice on your battery cables."

Sam shrugged. "It will help with the rust."

The three of us collapsed on a beat-up couch that someone had had the foresight to prop against a wall. I held my dog up in a sort of toast to theirs. "Eat up, 'cause after tonight, everything changes."

All together we each took a big bite.

Alex winced and glanced at us both. "Hmm. That's a new flavor." It did *not* sound like he meant it in a good way.

Reggie rolled his eyes lightly. "Chill, man. Street dogs haven't killed us yet."

As far as "famous last words" go? Those were kind of on the nose.

We were gone before the screech of the ambulance's siren pierced the air.

1

Julie

My best friend, Flynn, is amazing: super caring, totally enthusiastic and supportive, and always up for fun. She's basically my other half, and there was no one I'd rather brave the crowded and competitive hallways of Los Feliz Performing Arts High School with. But hot dang, the girl is not someone who shies away from saying what's on her mind.

She cornered me this morning just beside my locker. I was battling with the combination, head down, trying to blend into the walls under the brim of my baseball cap, when she cozied over.

"Hey, underachiever," she sang, the glint in her eyes telling me she was (mostly) joking.

"Hey, disappointment." Best friend or not, I could serve it right back with the best of them.

Flynn cocked a hip and peered at me, curious. "Okay, I know you don't want me to ask, but have you decided what you're gonna do today?"

Had I decided? No. Spent hours the night before, tossing and turning in my bed, considering, yes. But that was way different from deciding. "I'll know in the moment," I bluffed, trying to sound more confident than I felt.

Flynn was *not* impressed. "Really? That's all you're giving me? Jules, Mrs. Harrison said this is your last chance."

As if I needed a reminder. I swallowed. I hadn't been able to bring myself to play the piano since my mother died a year ago. Music was her passion, and it was the thing that connected us. Every time I sat down at the bench to prepare, my chest felt tight and fluttery. Playing piano now that Mom was gone? It felt pointless. Worse than pointless . . . it felt like a *betrayal* of her, and her spirit.

But it was getting harder and harder to justify my place in a *performing arts school specialty program* when I couldn't seem to bring myself to, well . . . *perform.*

"I know," I said to Flynn, more matter-of-factly than I was feeling inside. "I was there."

I expected some tough love from Flynn, but she'd turned, caught on something going on over my shoulder. "Ugh, what's *she* handing out?"

I turned to see who she was looking at. *Carrie.* Of course. Swanning down the halls like she owned the school. Her golden hair tumbled angelically over her shoulders and, of course, somehow the fluorescent lighting of the hallways cast a perfect shining spotlight on her expertly coordinated outfit.

You know how in those old movies from the nineties, there's always that classic "mean girl" type? Blonde, cute, always dressed head to toe in the latest trends—says whatever's on her mind, no matter how nasty it might seem?

Yeah, *that* type. That was Carrie, to a T. Never mind that we'd actually grown up as friends—those days were long gone.

And judging from the smug smile on her lips right now, she was currently in the throes of planning and/or executing something particularly diabolical. Or if not necessarily *diabolical*, at least it would be annoying. And it seemed to involve printed flyers.

"Here you go," she said, gliding up to me and thrusting a flyer in my face. She ignored Flynn's disgusted look. "My group's performing at the spirit rally tomorrow." She gave me a withering once-over. "I'm sure you guys have nothing better to do."

Ugh, Carrie's group, Dirty Candi. Flynn and I always assumed that her dad gave her music career a boost. (Not that we blamed her for taking it.) Her father was Trevor Wilson, the famous musician. He's, like, a *huge* star. One of his songs was even featured in a car commercial! *My* dad said it was selling out a little bit, but . . . come on! A commercial! Anyway, I figured Carrie's always had her dad in her corner . . . and she and *I* have always been in opposite corners of the ring.

Still, no matter how much support Carrie seemed to get from her dad, it was nothing compared to my mom and me. She was my biggest champion.

But there's that word again: *was*. And since she died, it's become hard for me to . . . I don't know, face the music? But, like, literally.

Flynn threw a look at Carrie. "Oh my gosh, Carrie, thanks." Her voice dripped with scorn.

Carrie glared at her. "Oh my gosh, Flynn, don't bother coming."

Carrie's boyfriend, Nick, appeared and wrapped an arm around her shoulders, glancing at me as if to apologize for her attitude.

I gave a small, imperceptible shrug. There was no apologizing for Carrie. And *no* accounting for what Nick saw in her. It was so wrong, the two of them together.

I watched them move off down the hall. But that imperceptible moment between Nick and me? Yeah, not as subtle as I'd hoped. Flynn doesn't miss a beat.

She gave me a look. "Nick? Still? You know those two are gonna get married and have a bunch of unholy babies."

"Nick's a sweetheart," I protested.

"Too bad his girlfriend's a spoiled brat." Flynn nudged

me. "There's that smile." She linked an arm through mine. "Now, let's go prove everyone wrong."

The music room at Los Feliz High School was more like a cathedral than a performance space; for everyone in our arts program, music was a kind of religion. The program was competitive, audition-only, and we all had to earn our spot here. We had to keep earning it, too, throughout our time in school.

Meanwhile, my time? Well, it was running out. And there was a line of students out the proverbial door who'd be thrilled to take my spot if I didn't find a way to get my muse back. The principal had made my options crystal clear—it was now or never. If I couldn't play, I couldn't stay.

When Flynn and I entered the room, Nick was finishing up his own showcase: Smiling that easy, open grin of his, he was absolutely shredding it, wailing classical music on his electric guitar. It was the opposite of what you'd expect to hear from that instrument—which made it totally Nick. He fit in with everyone, all the time, and he made things that felt worlds apart, at least to the rest of us, converge seamlessly. *There* was a guy who never had a problem tapping into his muse.

As he finished his piece and gave a little bow, the room broke into applause. Carrie sat front and center, cheering loudly and beaming at her boyfriend. Mrs. Harrison, the music teacher, stepped forward.

"Nice job, Nick. Almost as impressive as your last game against Glendale."

(What did I say about Nick being good at *everything*?)

She searched the room, resting her gaze on me. "Okay, that leaves us with one last performance. Julie?"

It felt like the eyes of every single person in the room were trained on me. I swallowed; my throat was dry.

Flynn leaned in. "You got this," she whispered.

I cleared my throat, taking off my hat and shaking off my coat. I walked toward the center of the room, where the piano awaited me, like I was walking a plank. Every footstep I took thundered in my ears. As I moved past her, Carrie leaned over to whisper something to Nick, but I tried to shut her (and the rest of the room) out.

One step at a time, I told myself, trying to channel some of Flynn's confidence. *You can do this.*

Sit at the bench. Hands over the keys. Foot on the pedal.

I tried, I really did. I saw it in my head: I began to play. Just a few bars, the notes sounding stiff and uncertain for a minute. But then it was like . . . I don't know, sort of like coming alive, like a big overhead stretch when you first wake up in the morning. It felt open, and free, and . . . *right.*

Until Mom's face appeared in my mind, too, bright and loving, blocking out everything else in the room.

Back in real life, my fingers froze as a bowling ball sank to the base of my stomach. I couldn't do this. I didn't belong here. Not anymore.

Without a word, I jumped up, grabbed my things, and ran from the room.

Behind me, I could hear all my classmates reacting. Some were surprised—gasping, murmuring to one another. I didn't dare glance at Flynn. I couldn't stand her worrying or feeling sorry for me. And above all the whispers rose Carrie's voice, clear and as sharp as glass. She was eating this all up, like I would have expected.

"Is this the part when we clap?"

Flynn caught up to me in the stairwell. "Julie!" Her voice echoed against the walls, tinny and high with worry.

I stopped and turned. What was there to say?

"They're gonna kick you out of music." She said it plainly. Flynn and I were always straight with each other.

So I was going to be straight with her now, too. I took a deep breath. "I'm done, Flynn."

I ran off before she could say anything else.

2

Julie

After the disastrous day I'd had at school, all I wanted was to be at home, curled up in my coziest sweats, the rest of the world blocked out and pushed away. Right away, I got comfortable at the kitchen counter. I was trying to shut out the memory of my humiliation, which meant I had my notebook out. I told myself I was "just" doing some freewriting—it wasn't, like, song lyrics or anything.

I definitely wasn't writing music. I mean, that would be the last thing I would go to for a little inner peace these days.

I heard footsteps and looked up to see Dad enter the room. He was a photographer, which meant that his working hours were all over the place. Quickly, I slid my notebook shut. He didn't need to know about my "freewriting."

"Oh, good, you're home," he said. "I was just about to go watch your brother's game. I've had photo shoots all day, haven't even had a chance to eat. But—I did get a call today."

Busted. "Yeah, I figured as much." What would he say, now that I was officially kicked out of the music program at school? I braced myself.

"It was from my Realtor friend."

"Oh." So, not the school, then. That bought me a little more time to figure out how I was going to break the bad news. *Bright side.*

You got kicked out of music, Jules, my inner voice chimed in. *There is no bright side here.*

"She said if we're still serious about selling, she wants me to take some pictures for the website."

Pictures. For the website. Meaning, pictures of our house, which would soon be listed online as "for sale." Our beautiful, comfortable, bright blue craftsman that I'd lived in my whole life. Did I *want* to move? I couldn't say for sure. But the memories here . . . They were powerful. *Painful.* I felt Mom everywhere . . . and especially in her music studio. The space was filled with ghosts: of her music, of her passion. I couldn't even bring myself to set foot in it these days.

Dad had a point to make, though. "Which means we need to clean up the house, get rid of some stuff."

"Let me know how that goes."

"Nice try." Dad smirked. "I was hoping we could all help out." He took a deep breath, so tentative I knew immediately what was coming. "Maybe you could . . . tackle Mom's studio?"

There it is. For the second time that day, all the air left the room as my stomach clenched. I took a deep breath of my own and tried not to react.

"Tu eres la experta," he said. "You're the expert. Your brother and I wouldn't even know where to start." He paused, waiting to see if I'd chime in. When I didn't, he continued. "*If* you're ready. I know it's going to be hard, but we can do it."

My eyes welled. Dad was doing his best to fill Mom's place for us, here at home . . . and he was missing her, too. I was a disappointment at music school, okay. But that didn't mean I couldn't try a little harder in other places, at other times, to do my part. "No, it's all right," I said. "Maybe I'll start tonight."

"Gracias, mija," Dad said. "And don't forget the loft. Those old instruments that were here when we moved in need a home."

"Mom would like that," I agreed.

"Yeah. Why she kept those, I'll never know . . ." He trailed off as he glanced at his watch. "Shoot, I'm gonna be late for your brother's game." He patted at his pockets, then glanced around the room, a familiar panicked look coming over his face.

"Under the mail," I said.

He reached under the pile and swiftly pulled out his keys. "Gracias, mi amor."

He moved to the door. He was trying so hard. I knew I had to tell him about school. "Dad?"

"Yeah?" His face was so expectant . . . I couldn't do it.

"Nada. Forget it," I said. "Just tell Carlos good luck."

We could all use a little good luck around here these days.

———

The moon had risen by the time I headed out to Mom's studio. Our backyard was cast in a celestial glow, and the sound of crickets chirping surrounded me as I made my way to the converted garage. For the second time in one day, I found myself walking as slowly as possible, trying to put off an unpleasant moment. But here I was and there they were: the barn doors that opened into the studio. There was nothing left to do but go inside.

I took a deep breath and opened the doors.

I flicked on the lights first thing. I saw it right in the center of the space, just like always: Mom's piano. It was draped in a cloth, looking just like the ghost of Mom's music that dominated this whole room. Everything was still just as we'd left it—just as *she'd* left it: a ratty old sofa bed covered in a sheet, the colorful floor pillows and throw rugs that kept the place from looking like a garage and more like someone's personal creative hideout.

Too personal: The window curtains were faded, but they were printed with dahlias, Mom's favorite flower. The sight of them made my stomach sink.

I ran a finger along the surface of a side table, tracing a line in the dust that had gathered. Her teacup was still there, and the spoon she'd been using the last time . . .

The last time.

"Sorry I haven't been in here, Mom," I said into the emptiness.

I pulled the sheet off the sofa and then removed the piano cover. The baby grand was, miraculously, still gleaming, as though Mom had been around taking care of it all this time. A few handwritten pages of sheet music fluttered to the ground. I hovered one hand over the key lid, thinking about lifting it.

Then I pulled my hand back again, sighing.

I moved to the loft, just like Dad had asked. It was nothing but clutter: a few dusty old guitar cases, a drum kit, some random storage boxes, and a very old shoebox that I didn't remember. A scratched-up CD in one corner caught my eye, resting against a boom box. (We were probably the only house in the neighborhood that still had a CD player.) The case read, *Sunset Curve demo.*

I know I was supposed to be cleaning. But in that

moment, I couldn't help myself. It was like some force had come over me—maybe it was Mom herself?—telling me to play the CD. So I cued it up in the boom box and watched, waiting, as the disc spun. It wasn't long before the room filled with the sound of soulful guitar rock. What was it the principal had said about my music classes? Oh, right: *Now or never.*

Just like the chorus of this song.

It felt weirdly meaningful. Goose bumps broke out on my arms. The air felt charged, like it does before a storm. Suddenly, the music cut off. All I could hear was the sound of wind, like it was rushing down a tunnel. Louder and louder still . . . until:

BOOM!

An ethereal ball of light *exploded* into the room! Then another, and then one more, each seemingly brighter than the last. I blinked, barely able to process what I was seeing. Slowly, the shapes materialized into . . .

Three . . . *guys?*

Correction: three *cute* guys.

(Which I know didn't really take away from the weirdness of the whole situation, but I couldn't help but notice anyway.) One was blond; one had dark, wavy hair and dark eyes; and one looked . . . well, he looked exactly like he should be the lead of a boy band. I couldn't describe it any better than that. He had floppy brown hair and blue eyes that—right now, at least—looked as confused as I was feeling.

Get in line, buddy, I thought, my heart popcorning in my chest. *Who were these guys, and what the heck were they doing in my mom's studio? What do I do? Call the police? Call for Dad?* I couldn't do anything—I was glued in place, paralyzed by shock.

And then, Floppy-Hair spoke. "Whoa, how did we get back here?"

It was too much, hearing those words come from his mouth. He *spoke*. *Words*. Out loud, and I heard them.

I opened my mouth to ask something—anything!—but all that came out was a panicked scream.

The boys turned like they were noticing me in the room with them for the first time. Then they started screaming right back at me.

3

Julie

The guys—the ones who appeared basically *out of thin air*—must have gotten over the shock quicker than I did. I was still screaming when the blond one finally winced, plugging his ears with his fingers.

"Please stop," he begged, straining to be heard over me.

I did, but it wasn't easy. "Who *are* you?" I demanded, quickly grabbing a cross off the wall and holding it out, like I was trying to ward off a pack of vampires. "Why are you in my mom's studio?"

"Your mom's studio? This is *our* studio," Floppy-Hair said, with a crooked smile that suggested he was sort of joking. But then he took a closer look around. "I mean, sure, the grand piano's new . . . and the plants . . . and the lack of trash . . ." He trailed off. "Give me a second."

He moved to his friends, making a little huddle. I tried

not to eavesdrop, but the garage isn't all that big, and the acoustics were great. (That was part of what made it such a good music studio.)

"What's happening?" Floppy asked. "How'd she get her stuff in here so fast?"

"Maybe she's a witch," the dark-haired boy put in.

"There's no such thing as witches."

"You sure?" Floppy countered. "'Cause I used to think there was no such thing as ghosts."

Ghosts. I shivered. That was what you called it when people appeared out of thin air. I gripped that cross more tightly. *This is really happening, Jules.*

Ghosts. There were *ghosts* in my mother's studio. Self-proclaimed.

Floppy shrugged, like he was considering this. "So we're going with witch?"

The blond looked slightly panicked. "No! She's just scared. Let someone with a softer touch handle this." He turned to me, sincere. "Why are you in our studio?"

My mind raced. *Their* studio?! I lunged forward toward him, swiping at him with the cross. But instead of making contact with the guy, the cross passed right through his body!

"Oh *my god*!" I shrieked. "How did you do that?"

He spoke slowly, like I was a little kid. "Since you're obviously struggling with this: We're ghosts. Three ghosts just happy to be home. And thanks for the plants—really brightens up the place."

I wanted to protest; I really, really did. But there was that whole thing about my hand having gone straight through his body. It was hard to ignore.

"We're also in a band," Floppy added. "Called Sunset Curve."

"Tell your friends," Dark-Hair chimed in. Next thing you know, he'd be offering me a band T-shirt or something.

Floppy stepped forward, looking earnest. "Last night was supposed to be a big night for us. It was gonna change our lives."

"I'm pretty sure it did," the blond quipped, totally deadpan.

Deadpan. No pun intended.

Ghosts. We were still talking about *ghosts* here. The only reason it wasn't *totally* insane was because the alternative seemed to be their suggestion that I was a witch. And I knew *that* wasn't the case.

Well, there was one way to investigate this. Keeping one eye on the boys, I took a giant step back and pulled my phone out of my back pocket.

I typed in *Sunset Swerve*, tapping frantically on the screen. "*This is crazy*," I whispered to myself.

"What are you doing? What's that?" Floppy asked, craning his neck to see.

Okay, what? Had these guys never seen a cell phone before?

26

"It's my phone," I said, incredulous. Then, to myself again, "Nope, stop talking to them, they are not real. There's no such thing as cute ghosts."

"You think we're cute?" Dark-Hair asked, looking hopeful.

I ignored him while the blond tried to peek at my phone. "Who are you calling?"

I sighed. "I'm googling Sunset Swerve."

All together they shouted back at me, "Sunset *Curve*!"

Sure, whatever, I thought. But before I could finish thinking it, the internet had brought back some disturbing answers.

"Whoa. There *is* a Sunset Curve—not 'swerve,'" I said. The boys looked briefly triumphant. "And you guys did die." At this, they looked less excited. "But not last night." I looked up, not sure how to break the news to them. "You died . . . twenty-five years ago."

The room went still. Then Dark-Hair—the internet told me his name was Reggie—stepped forward, upset.

"What? That's impossible. After we floated out of that ambulance, all we did was go to that weird, dark room where Alex cried."

Alex—the blond—stiffened. "Uh, I believe we were *all* pretty upset."

"And it was only for, like, an hour," Floppy-Hair— Luke, according to Google—put in. "And then we showed up here."

It all sounded . . . well, I couldn't say how it sounded, exactly. This being my first experience with *ghosts*. "I'm just telling you what my phone says." I held it out to them. "See—you died in 1995, when you were seventeen. Now it's 2020."

"This is the future?" Reggie said, taking another look around the studio.

Weirdest. Day. Ever.

"Wait, wait. Hold up," Alex protested. "So it *has* been twenty-five years? I was crying for *twenty-five* years? How is that possible?"

"Well, you *are* very emotional," Reggie said.

"No, I'm not!" Alex replied, totally emotional.

We were so busy freaking out over the situation for all of our own personal reasons, no one noticed that Carlos— still in his baseball uniform—had entered the room until he spoke.

"Dad thought you might be out here," he said, looking at me while also eyeing the room. The boys froze in place. "Who are you talking to?"

"Can he see us?" Alex whispered to Reggie.

I watched Carlos carefully. I could tell from his body language that he definitely had no idea that the ghosts of a nineties boy band had materialized in the room with us. Which was good, since it would be a tough thing to explain away.

"No, he can't," I said to the boys, briefly forgetting that Carlos, too, would hear me say that.

Carlos looked at me like I was out of my mind. "What?"

"¿Qué tu quieres, Carlos?" I asked, defensive. Maybe I *was* out of my mind. Probably.

"I want a normal sister, for starters," he suggested. "Stop being weird and come eat." He left.

Once he was gone, I had to figure out what to do about these guys—these *ghosts*. And I had no clue.

"Look, I'm sorry for what happened to you guys, truly. But this isn't your studio anymore," I told them. "You have to leave."

And *I* had to eat dinner and pretend everything about this day was still completely and totally normal. Not that I had any idea how to do that.

———

I'd thought it was going to be hard keeping the news from Dad about music school. And it *was*. But that was nothing compared to the performance of a lifetime: normal Julie at family dinner with *a boy band of ghosts in her garage*.

We'd left our usual place set for Mom, clasping hands over her empty chair while Carlos said a quick grace. "Thank you for our leftovers and the power of the mighty microwave. Amen."

"Amen," Dad and I echoed.

Right away, Dad and Carlos dug in. I was distracted, though, pushing bites of food around the plate with my fork. My gaze kept wandering toward the garage; I was thinking about those boys . . . *Sunset Curve.* Why were they here? Like, on this earth again, after they died? But more specifically, why were they *here?* Like, in my house? (Well, technically, my garage, but you get what I mean.)

"Carlos said he found you in Mom's studio," Dad said, breaking into my thoughts. "You okay handling that?"

"She was out there talking to herself," Carlos said, snickering.

"I was rehearsing for a play," I shot back. To Dad I just said, "I'm fine, really."

"Hello-hello!"

It was Aunt Victoria, swinging by uninvited to be sure we hadn't gone feral since losing Mom. Her intentions were good, but that didn't make her unannounced drop-ins any less stressful. Having her around just called attention to the ways we *weren't* normal anymore. We sprang into action, clearing away Mom's place from the table before Aunt Victoria rounded the corner into the room.

Come to think of it, in a lot of ways, we were all pretty good at pretending to be normal. But it was just that: pretending.

"Spaghetti again?" She eyed our plates. "That's too bad. I brought you my arroz con pollo y pasteles."

"Gracias, Tía, it smells great," I said.

"You can have it tomorrow," she said, decisive. "I can't let you have leftover pasta every night. My sister would kill me, que en paz descanse."

An awkward silence fell over the table as we all tried not to look toward Mom's empty seat. "Are things going better?" she asked.

Dad looked up, bright. "Yep, Julie actually started cleaning out Rose's studio. Hopefully, we can get the house on the market and get some offers."

"I like the sound of that. Moving from here will only help you move on. You've got to rip off that Band-Aid and get the pain over with." She turned to me. "And now that you're no longer in the music program, you can concentrate on the classes that matter."

Dad shot me a stunned look, and I glanced away. None of this escaped Aunt Victoria, whose dark eyes flashed. "You read the email from school, too, right?"

"Of course," Dad covered. "We're still discussing it."

"Pues," Aunt Victoria said, obviously wanting to escape the awkwardness that had come over the room, "if I hurry, I can make my Pilates class. ¡Los quiero muchos, mijos!"

The front door slammed shut behind her, and then Carlos raced to fill the void and come to my rescue. "So . . . who wants to hear about my slide into home—"

"Not now, Carlos," Dad said.

Carlos looked at me. "I tried." He grabbed his own plate and walked out, leaving me to face Dad—and the music—alone.

"Why didn't you tell me?" Dad demanded. "I had to lie to your aunt."

"Sorry." I swallowed. "I was going to tell you after dinner."

"Uh-huh." Dad was not convinced.

"I don't know why we haven't taken her off the school's email list."

"Because of days like this when I'm too busy to even look at email. And your aunt helping me isn't what this is about. I know going to those classes has been difficult, but you still like music, don't you?"

How could I answer that? Did I still like music? It was the most important thing in the world to me. But also the most painful. "I don't know. Maybe."

Dad was quiet for a moment. "Mi amor," he said at last, "I know we talked about how hard memories can be, but they're all we have now. Every day, you and your brother remind me of your mom. It's like she's still here. And I love it. If you give yourself a chance, you might get there, too."

He so didn't get it. "Sorry, but I just can't force myself to feel music. It's like that part of me is gone."

Just as I said it, I heard a sound fill the air. It was live music. And it was coming from . . . the garage? Was it Sunset Curve playing in the studio?

32

Carlos reappeared in the dining room. "What's that?" he asked. *He could hear it, too?*

Think fast.

"Uh . . . I left the stereo on. I'll get it."

Before anyone could say anything, I ran to the garage.

4

Julie

It was a full-on ghost jam session.

That was the only way to describe what I saw when I got to the garage. The boys had somehow managed to get ahold of their instruments, and they were rocking out. That was the music that I'd heard—no, that *we'd* heard— in the dining room.

"Guys! Guys!" I burst in, flustered. "Or, ghosts. Whatever—stop!"

At last, they noticed me over their own sound and stopped.

"The whole neighborhood can hear you," I said, breathless. "I thought I told you to leave."

"Wait," Luke said, startled. "You heard us playing?"

"Yes! And so did my dad and my brother!" How were they not seeing the problem here?

"So, only *you* can see us," Alex said, working it through. "But everyone can hear us play? What kind of ghosts are we?"

"Who cares? *People can hear us play!*" Luke said. He and Reggie high-fived, super excited.

"Yes! We may be dead, but our music isn't!" Reggie said.

These guys—*ghosts*—so weren't seeing the big picture.

Luke and Reggie were taking off their guitars when my father wandered into the studio.

"Dad!" *Could he see them?*

"Hey," he said. "Just making sure you're okay."

Okay, that answered my question.

He looked around, taking in the band's instruments. "Is this all the junk that was in the loft?"

"Junk?" Luke echoed, hurt.

"Actually," Dad said, moving closer to take a better look at the drum set, "some of this stuff is in pretty good shape. Maybe we could make a couple of bucks."

"What?" Alex cried, devastated. "Stop touching my drums." He looked at me. "Tell him to stop touching my drums!"

"I liked that song you had on," Dad said.

"We're Sunset Curve," Luke said, proud.

"Tell your friends," Reggie added.

"It was . . . just an old CD I found," I said.

"Well, it's nice that you're listening to music again," Dad said. "Play whatever you want out here, whenever you want."

"Aw, that's nice," Reggie said.

I glared at him. "Stay out of this."

"Oh, perdón, mi amor," Dad said, backing up. "I'm sorry. I didn't mean to push. It's just . . ."

"No! Not you," I said. At his confused expression, I added, "I mean . . . I'll just be a second."

"Of course," he replied. "And we'll figure out this music program thing, okay?"

"Thanks, Dad."

He went back into the house, leaving me and the ghosts to give huge sighs of relief.

(Wait, did ghosts sigh?)

"Didja hear that?" Reggie asked, once the coast was truly clear. "He liked our song."

"He's a dad," Alex said. "He doesn't count."

"Why can't you just be normal ghosts and hang out in an old mansion?" I asked. "I hear Pasadena's nice."

I didn't stick around to hear their answer.

———

I hadn't made it any farther than the driveway before Luke materialized in front of me. It was very disconcerting. "Aaah!" I was doing a lot of screaming tonight.

"Stop that," I told him, once I'd calmed down. "I'm serious."

"Sorry," he said.

"What do you want?" I asked.

"I know this is all completely insane, but you *do* know how awesome this is. People can hear us play," he said.

"Yeah," I agreed. "But I've just had a really, *really* awful day. I have to go."

He ghost-stepped a little closer to me, trying to keep me from leaving. "Well, I'm sorry you had a bad day, but three guys just found out they had a bad twenty-five years. And *then* they found out the one thing they lived for in the first place? They can still do. That's pretty rad."

He had a point. And his eyes were trained on mine, piercing.

"You're right," I relented. "It's just . . ."

"Your bad day. I know. Sorry we came into your life. But what I just felt in there? Made *me* actually feel alive again."

His words hit me, hard.

"We *all* felt alive," he went on. "And you can kick us out if you want, but we're not giving up music. We can *play* again. That's a gift no musician would turn down. You should understand that. Clearly, your mom's into music."

I should *understand that.* And yet, playing was the one thing I couldn't do. "Was," I corrected him. "She passed away." I still couldn't say it without a lump welling up in the back of my throat.

"Oh, sorry." Luke *did* look sorry.

"We didn't know."

I flinched, realizing that Alex and Reggie had just appeared in the driveway with us, too. "It's okay," I said.

For a beat, we were quiet. No one seemed to know what to say or do next.

But I had a question. One that I knew might have a painful answer. And yet, I couldn't help but ask it. "You guys haven't ever . . . seen her anywhere, have you? You know—wherever you came from." Because if ghosts did exist . . . maybe that meant I'd see my mother again, someday? Somehow?

"Nope," Alex said. "You're the first person we've seen. But we're . . . so sorry for your loss." He looked genuinely sad for me.

"Thanks," I said, meaning it. "And I'm sorry I got so mad. You guys are good."

"And that was twenty-five years of rust getting knocked off," Luke pointed out, grinning.

"Do you play the piano, too?" Reggie asked.

"No," I said quickly. "I don't play. That was all my mom's stuff in there."

"Oh. Then she was a pretty good songwriter," Luke said.

"She was," I agreed. Then, "How would you know?"

"There's a song on the piano. If it was hers, she had talent."

If it was hers, she had talent. She did have talent. And I missed her more than even music could express.

If she were here right now, seeing these ghosts—connecting with their music . . . well, I knew what she'd want me to do. To say.

"I guess . . . if you need a place to stay, you can stay in there," I said, nodding toward the studio. "There's a bathroom in the back, and the couch turns into a bed . . . if you still use any of that stuff."

"Dibs on the shower," Reggie called. "What?" he asked, at my look. "Ghosts can't like showers? And even sometimes the occasional bath?"

I shook my head. "This? Is too weird."

5

Alex

Poof. Seconds after Julie walked off, Luke told us he wanted to show us something, and we concentrated until everything went dark and cloudy. When the darkness broke, the guys and I were on the roof of the Orpheum, looking down at the crowd below.

"I know being dead isn't our first choice, but it sure is easy getting around," Luke said, obviously pleased with himself for getting here.

I wasn't so sure about that. It wasn't such a smooth transition for me. The being-dead part—which was still totally upsetting—and the poofing-around thing, which wasn't as easy as it looked.

"Why would we come *here*?" I asked Luke, upset. "It's just a painful reminder of where we never got to play."

Right now, it felt like *everything* was a painful reminder.

I didn't remember much—at least, not clearly—about that room where we'd been before this. But knowing we were, you know, *dead*, had been hard enough to process. So now, being back?

On the one hand: Cool. Welcome to the next level. So there *was* such a thing as the afterlife, after all.

On the other hand: We were still, you know, actually *dead*. Our families and friends had grown up, moved on. And no one but one random girl could see or talk to us.

And meanwhile, none of us had any idea *why* we were back.

So the jury was still out on whether being here, now, was good news or bad. And in the meantime, like I said: It was all a little bit painful.

"But the game isn't over yet," Luke said, poofing out and reappearing down on the street. Reggie and I followed suit.

"Let's go listen to some music, see how many clubs we can hit before sunrise." It was what we'd do back when we were . . . alive. And it was hard to say no. We didn't have anything better to do, and a little bit of normal "life" wasn't the worst idea. We started to move through the crowd, still weirded out by the way we could just slip past all the living people, unnoticed (even though it was kind of convenient, too). Not to mention the fact that the living people could literally slip *through* us.

Suddenly, though, a body slammed into me. Solid as

wood. He was tall and dressed like something out of an old movie—a long cape, a top hat—and the impact was so surprising it almost knocked me over. "Hey!"

The man turned and grinned at me. His eyes were an electric shade of blue and his smile had a hint of . . . menace to it. He tipped his hat to me—like, literally—and then vanished into the crowd.

Who—or what—*was that?*

Nobody else saw that weird guy, so I decided to keep it to myself for the rest of the night. Enough bizarre things had already happened to us that day. We hit each and every club, just like Luke suggested. Being a ghost did seem to make things kind of . . . I don't know, *efficient.* Going to the clubs as ghosts wasn't the same as going when we were alive—we couldn't talk to anyone, for one thing. But it was nice to be out and around people. Even if those people couldn't see us.

We had just poofed back to the garage as the sun began to rise. All around us, it felt like the city was quiet, just starting to wake up. But then Julie approached the studio. She looked nervous but wide-awake, like she'd maybe been awake for a little while now.

For a second, we hovered outside, not sure what was going on. Then we watched as Julie approached her mother's piano.

We didn't mean to eavesdrop, I swear. We didn't go into the studio. But we understood—maybe better than anyone else ever could—what this moment meant. Julie was coming back to music. The way she'd looked in her mother's space yesterday when we showed up . . . (I mean, before she saw us and freaked out). She'd been in awe. I knew, then, that this was a girl to whom music meant everything. Even if she *said* she didn't play.

We didn't want to move, to take a breath (even if, technically, ghosts don't breathe), because we didn't want to ruin this moment for her.

Julie sat down at the bench and took her mother's sheet music—the same music we'd been looking at the day before—and stood it up against the piano. She closed her eyes and took a deep breath, like she was maybe saying some silent prayer, inside.

Then she began to play.

The thing was: When we saw that sheet music? We knew the music was good.

But when Julie played, that music was beyond. It was *transcendent.* It was like nothing we'd ever heard. If ghosts could get goose bumps, I would have, and looking at Reggie and Luke, I knew they were feeling the same way.

The melody built beneath her fingers, her emotion swelling with the rising chords. She began to sway her head side to side, feeling it . . . and then she began to sing.

Here's the one thing / I want you to
know / You got someplace to go /
Life's a test yes / But you go toe
to toe / You don't give up, no
you grow

And use your pain / 'Cause it
makes you you / Though I wish / I
could hold you through it / I know
it's not the same / You got livin'
to do / And I just want you to do it

So get up get out relight that
spark / You know the rest by heart

Wake up wake up if it's all you do /
Look out look inside of you / It's
not what you lost / It's what you'll gain /
Raising your voice to the rain

Wake up your dream and make it true /
Look out, look inside of you / It's not
what you lost / Relight that spark /
Time to come out of the dark

Wake up / wake up

Better wake those demons / Just

look them in the eye / No reason
not to try

Life can be a mess / I won't let it
cloud my mind / I'll let my fingers fly

And I use the pain / 'Cause it's
part of me / And I'm ready to power
through it

Gonna find the strength / Find the
melody / 'Cause you showed me how to
do it

Get up get out relight that
spark / You know the rest by heart

Tears rose in Julie's eyes as she repeated the chorus of the song, but she didn't stop playing. I felt a little teary, too. Her voice was so soulful, the song was so haunting . . .

I couldn't remember the last time I felt so moved by music that wasn't actually my own.

6

Alex

The final note of Julie's powerful song hung in the air.
Julie was slumped at the piano, drained. At some point,
we'd poofed through the studio walls—like I said, we
didn't mean to eavesdrop, but listening to Julie play was
mesmerizing. Now I approached her, but Luke pulled me
back. We poofed to the driveway.

"Why'd you stop me? Julie needed a hug," I said.

"A ghost hug isn't the feel-good moment you think
it is," Luke pointed out. "Trust me, what Julie needs is pri-
vacy." He stood up straighter, thinking things through.

"First thing we're gonna do," he said, running
his hand through his hair, "when we get the courage to
go in there—is ask Julie why she lied about playing the
piano."

"And maybe tell her how amazing she was?" I prompted.

"Of course," Luke said.

"She's the bomb. I got ghost bumps," Reggie said.

Before I could reply, another girl came storming down the driveway.

"Whoa, drama," I said. *Yikes. A lot of feelings going on around here.*

Luke nodded and gave a knowing look. "Now we *definitely* can't go in there."

"But we *can* listen," Reggie said.

We poofed back into the loft. Julie sat at the piano, her eyes dry now. Her friend was a tornado of energy.

"Carlos told me you were out here. We need to talk."

"Flynn, are you okay?" Julie asked. *Okay, so her friend's name is Flynn.*

"No!" the friend—*Flynn*—exploded. "I'm not okay. You got kicked out of music! I've been up all night thinking about what I was gonna say. Might've drank seven sodas, but I need to get this out." She paced, which made a lot more sense in light of the information about the soda.

"Wait," Julie tried to interject. "I have something to tell—"

"No, it's my time to talk." Flynn cut her off. "You *can't* give up music. That would be a tragedy. Your music is a gift, so you're basically canceling Christmas! And I *love* Christmas."

Julie tried again. "Flynn, I—"

"Uh-uh. When we were six, we promised to be in a band together. Double Trouble."

"I never agreed to that name."

"That's not the point!" Flynn's voice rose. "Jules, if you leave the music program, we'll be apart forever. That's just what happens. We'll have different lives and make new friends . . . the only contact we'll have is liking each other's posts on Instagram."

What-stagram? Some parts of the future were seriously confusing.

"And every time I hit that little heart," Flynn said, choking up slightly, "*my* heart will be breaking because my best friend left me." She finished, finally, crossing her arms over her chest and looking at Julie, expectant.

"Now can I talk?" Julie asked.

Flynn rolled her eyes. "Fine."

"I just played the piano and sang again."

Flynn's eyes flew open in shock. "What?! Why didn't you say so?"

"I was trying, but then your seven sodas kicked in," Julie said, laughing.

Flynn swept Julie up in a giant hug. "I'm so happy for you! And for me! Look at you all, I don't know . . . *alive* again!"

It was the right word to use. When she was playing, Julie had truly come to life. I knew what that felt like.

"What made you play?" Flynn asked.

"Uh, well, yesterday I found a song my mom wrote for me," Julie said.

"Whoa."

"I know. I was afraid to play it, because everything about music reminds me of her. Then I woke up this morning realizing that's why I *should* play it. To keep her memory alive." Julie's eyes were shining.

Flynn grabbed Julie and hugged her again. Then suddenly, she broke away. "We need to show Mrs. Harrison you can play again," she said, determined. "So you can stay in the program and my life doesn't become the very sad picture I just painted for you."

Flynn grabbed Julie's backpack and started escorting her toward the studio door. "My girl's back," she proclaimed, proud. "Double Trouble lives again!"

"Not our band name," Julie said with a laugh as she left the garage.

After they were gone, Reggie was the first to speak. "Okay, but really. Why didn't Julie tell us she could shred on the piano?"

"And sing," Luke added, impressed. "That girl can *sing*."

"Didn't you hear what she said to her friend? It has to do with her mom. Must've been rough."

"Yeah," Luke said, "but now she's got music back in her life. Just like us."

"I'm not sure you can call what we have a 'life,'" I said with a huff. I started to rummage around in the boxes in the loft. "Hey, a lot of the stuff we left behind is still here." I grabbed one bag and passed it to Luke, who pulled a shirt out of it.

"Sweet. Clean shirt."

Well, there was another upside to our situation. At this point, we had to take what we could get.

After we had finished exploring in the loft, we poofed over to Seaside Park. It was a bright, sunny day, with people out enjoying the beach and that salty ocean smell in the air. Under any other circumstances, it would've been awesome.

Instead, we were staring in disbelief at the sight of a dingy-looking bike rental shack right on the spot where Reggie's house used to be. I shook my head, overwhelmed, while Luke kept a careful—and more caring than he'd probably ever admit—eye on Reggie.

"A bike shack . . ." Reggie mumbled, seeming numb. "Right where my house was. *Right here.*"

"I'm sorry, man," Luke said.

"They turned our neighbors' house into a noodle shop; why couldn't they turn mine into a pizzeria?" Reggie lamented.

I blinked, and suddenly, there it was—Luke's acoustic, right in his arms out of thin air, like it had been there all along!

"That was rad!" Reggie said. "How'd you do that?"

"I don't know," Luke said, clearly as stunned as we were. "I just wished I had it, and it was here."

Quickly, Reggie shut his eyes tight. "I wish I had a puppy."

Nothing.

He peeled one eye open toward the sky, hopeful. "A hamster?"

Nope.

Luke laughed, clapping him on the back reassuringly. "Don't worry, buddy. I've got something that will cheer you up." He began to strum his guitar.

I wanted to ignore him—Reggie and I both did—but the thing about Luke is that his enthusiasm is infectious. He's like the puppy that Reggie *didn't* get when he wished for one. "C'mon, Reginald," I coaxed, getting into it.

Luke counted us in, "*One, two, three four!*"

Cracking, Reggie began to move, riffing some lyrics to go with Luke's tune while I drummed on every available surface: benches, garbage can covers, my own knees . . . All around us, people began to hear the music. They obviously had no idea where it was coming from, but when the sound hit them, they began to smile. To dance. To *feel*.

Can you, 'a can you hear me? /

Loud and clear /

We gotta get, we gotta get ready /

'Cause it's been years /

Ooh, ooh, this band is back /

Ooh, ooh, this band is back

It wasn't what we expected. Or planned. And I didn't have any idea what was next for us. But in that moment, the truth of the song was all I needed. The band—*my family*—was back. And for now, it was enough.

7

Julie

If I thought playing piano was going to solve all my problems, I was in for a rude awakening. No matter how much Flynn pleaded my case, Mrs. Harrison was *not* here for it (and Flynn is super persistent, so that was saying something). Even after basically getting down on my knees and begging, things were what they were—I had bailed on my last chance to perform, and I'd lost my music spot at school. I didn't know if or when that would change.

So I wasn't in the greatest mood when I got home that afternoon, though I was really, *really* doing my best to concentrate on the positive. Dad was upset enough that I'd been kicked out of the program. I at least needed to put on a happy face.

When he walked into the kitchen, Dad was on his

laptop, frowning at something. Carlos was nearby, pecking away at a tablet.

"Whatcha working on?" I asked.

Dad gave a heavy sigh and pushed away from the table. "Now that the house is on the market, I need to add these photos to the website. Help me find the best ones."

I glanced at his screen and pointed at a few that captured the sunny exterior of our house on a perfect summer day. "These are really nice."

"Thanks," Dad said, toggling to another set of images. "These didn't turn out, though. The ones of your mom's studio. There are these weird spots in 'em, see? They're like orbs."

I looked. He was right: In the middle of each picture was a glowing, blobby image. The hairs on the back of my neck pricked up. *Are those what*—who—*I think they are?*

I wasn't the only one on alert at that. Carlos looked up from his tablet. "Orbs?" he repeated. "I've seen some freaky things about those on YouTube. People say they're ghosts. Do you think it's Mom? And she's made some friends?"

Oh, Carlos. If only Mom were the ghost in our garage.

"That's a nice thought," Dad said. "But there's no such thing as ghosts."

There were exactly three orbs in each image. Just like the three members of Sunset Curve. I had to somehow create a distraction. "I think someone's spending too much time on the internet," I said, dismissive. To my dad I just said, "We could just trash these."

I didn't wait for his response, instead clicking and dragging the incriminating photos into the trash.

"All right," Dad said, unconcerned. "I'll upload the good ones."

"Dad, I was thinking . . ." I started. "If we're just moving for me—we don't have to. I mean, if you and Carlos want to stay, I'm fine with that."

Was I, though? Fine? Maybe not completely. I'd lost my spot in the music program, and the fact that I'd played piano just this morning didn't change that. This house . . . it held so many . . . well, I didn't want to say *ghosts*. Too on the nose. But memories, yes. Important, but still painful.

And I wasn't totally ready to leave Sunset Curve behind. Not to mention all those painful, important memories? If I was playing music again, maybe I'd also taken a step toward embracing them again.

So, I was fine enough. For now.

Which meant that I belonged here. We all did. Together.

"I vote we stay," Carlos put in. "I don't want to have to clean out under my bed."

"Noted," Dad said, with a wry grin. Then he turned to me. "What made you have second thoughts?"

I shrugged. "I don't know, I guess a combination of

stuff. I know Tía said moving is moving on, but I don't think that's the answer."

"I agree with you there. Moving on has to come from inside. And one of us took a big step this morning." He gave me a meaningful look, and I realized he'd overheard me playing before school. I smiled back at him shyly. He understood—the painful memories *were* important. And they were the reason we needed to be in this house, keeping them close.

"All our memories of Mom are here, and we should be, too. Can we please stay?"

Dad shot Carlos a look, and Carlos clasped his hands together in his own begging gesture. "I guess the votes are in. We stay!"

I gave him a huge hug. "Te quiero, Papá."

"I love you, too, sweetie." He waved one hand toward Carlos. "You just gonna leave us hanging?"

Carlos rolled his eyes, but he joined us for a group hug. It felt nice—and *I* felt better than I had in a long time.

After a moment, Dad broke the silence. "Well, who's going to help me find my phone? I've got a real estate agent to call."

———

I ran back to my room to text Flynn the good news. But when I walked in, I was in for a major surprise.

Three surprises, to be exact. In the form of three

musical ghosts who *definitely* had no business poking around in my bedroom when I was out.

"What are you guys doing in here?" I demanded. Reggie was sprawled on my bed like he was planning to take a nap, Alex was trying desperately (but unsuccessfully) to pick up a picture frame from my nightstand, and Luke was poking the clutter all around my laptop.

"Uh . . ." Alex and Reggie stammered in unison.

"We were looking for the kitchen?" Luke tried.

"This can't happen. It's creepy," I said, definitive. I looked specifically at Reggie. "Get off my bed, please."

Reggie sat up, running his fingers through his mop of hair. Meanwhile, Luke was trying to lift up—*oh no*—my dream box.

"What's in this box?" he asked.

"That's off-limits," I said.

"Got it. So, girl stuff."

"Like, butterflies and glitter?" Reggie asked.

"It's none of your business," I snapped. "And yes, there may be some glitter."

"I did it!" Alex cried suddenly, triumphant. "I picked something up!"

I looked over to see him fumbling with my favorite picture of my mother—the one where she's standing in a field of dahlias. It slipped through his fingers, making me gasp—but landed safely on my bed, thank god.

". . . and I dropped it."

"Is that your mom?" Luke asked, looking at the picture.

"Yeah," I said, quickly picking up the frame and putting it back on my nightstand. "And this is my favorite picture of her. So if you break it, I'll break you."

"Sorry." Alex shrugged. "But I'm kinda unbreakable at this point."

I shook my head. "I don't get it. You guys can pick up your instruments, but you can't pick up other stuff?"

"It's just hard," Luke said. "For some reason our instruments are easy."

"Super easy," Reggie put in. "Look what we learned today." He closed his eyes in concentration, and after a minute his bass guitar came poofing into the room, slamming into his chest, and knocking him over backward.

"Yeah, that looked super easy," I noted.

"It's like I always thought," Luke said, his eyes lighting up. "Our instruments are attached to our souls."

"And sometimes to our belts," Reggie said, struggling to disentangle himself from the bass and mostly failing.

The door opened and Dad popped his head in. Even knowing he couldn't see them, the boys and I all froze. "Everything okay? Thought I heard you talking to someone."

"Nope," I said, scanning the room for a good explanation. "Must've been my laptop." *Which is closed.* "That I just closed."

"Okay," Dad said. He didn't seem totally convinced. "Let me know if you need anything."

After he was gone, the boys unfroze and started moving around normally again. (Well, as normal as was possible, given they were, you know, *ghosts*.)

"He looks like the kinda dad who likes to barbecue. He's got a good ribs recipe, doesn't he?"

I held a finger to my lips in a *shh* motion. "I don't know," I whispered. "But if you guys wanna talk to me, we should do it in the studio. He's already worried enough about me as it is."

Luke looked thoughtful. "He seems pretty cool. You should just tell him about us."

"You're kidding, right? This past year, everyone's been watching over me. Being super nice, like they're waiting for me to snap. If I tell my dad I met a ghost band, I'll be back to talking to Dr. Turner three days a week."

Nothing against Dr. Turner—therapy had definitely been helpful—but I was over being treated like everyone's fragile flower.

"I thought I said to leave that alone!" Out of the corner of my eye I realized Luke was investigating the dream box again.

"You shoulda never told me not to touch it. Now it's all I can think about."

I sighed. "It's just my dream box, okay? When I get an idea, I write it down to get it out of my head."

"Like lyrics?" he asked.

"They would be if I wrote music like I used to with my mom. Now it's just full of stuff that doesn't make me sad."

"But you do play. We heard you this morning," Alex said. Then, realizing, he flushed. "Uh . . ."

"So you were *there*, too?" I exploded. "Okay we need to set some boundaries right now. For starters, stay out of my room!"

"Fine, okay," Luke said, relenting.

"But before we do, I need to know," Alex said. "Did you get back into your music program?"

"No," I said, swallowing hard. "I didn't."

"That's crazy," Luke said. "Your voice, your piano playing. You're a human wrecking ball."

"Is that a compliment?" I asked.

Luke nodded, sincere. "You have the power to move people. To knock them off their feet. And there's no way you wouldn't get back into your music classes if your teacher heard you play."

Is that right? "Well, I asked her," I said. "And she said I have to wait until next semester."

"That was your first mistake," Luke said. "*Asking*. Sunset Curve booked gigs by *doing*. We went into ambush mode. We played in front of clubs. In back of clubs. We even played *book* clubs."

I looked at him. "Book clubs?"

"We didn't get any gigs out of that one," he admitted. "But we did get some pretty good snacks. I'm just saying, don't ask for permission. Just swing that wrecking ball of talent at your teacher's head and smash those stupid rules right out of her brain."

"This isn't a club," I reminded him. "It's a school. And your plan sounds violent."

"It's a closed door. You need to bust it open. Sorry, once I work with a metaphor, I own it. I learned *that* in book club."

"They're not just going to let me back in," I argued.

Luke stepped closer to me, lowering his voice so I could hear a new urgency creep in. "If getting back into music is what you want, then you gotta go for it. Learn from us—your tainted hot dog could be right around the corner."

Ugh, fine, point: Luke. "I don't even have anything prepared."

Luke pulled a sheet of paper out of his back pocket. It was music. "It's called 'Bright,'" he said. "It's a Sunset Curve song I wrote that we never recorded. It's perfect for your range."

I looked at the music, then back at Luke.

"All it needs is a little piano," he said.

The other boys looked at me, expectant.

I turned the thought over in my head.

It wasn't the worst idea I'd ever heard. And Luke was right—the song would be perfect. But I'd just sat down at the piano for the first time in ages *this morning*.

Was I really ready for a musical ambush? And if I was, would the school be ready for me?

8

Julie

"Look who spent all her daddy's money on new costumes and Katy Perry's choreographer," Flynn grumbled.

> Made moves / On the rise now / Run
> stuff get a piece of that pie now /
> We're the best, no doubt / Check it
> out yeah we make 'em say wow

But Flynn's sarcasm about Carrie's performance at the high school spirit assembly was lost on me. Carrie's band, Dirty Candi, *was* as polished as any professional pop band. The school auditorium was decked out in balloons and banners in sky blue, maroon, and white, our school colors, which was dizzying enough. When you added in Dirty Candi's theatrical lights that they'd brought in special? It felt less like a high school rally and more like a Super Bowl halftime show.

In short? Carrie was going to be a tough act to follow. But I had to do it.

"Man, I miss high school." It was Reggie, in my ear.

"What are you guys doing here?" I hissed. They'd helped with the planning and provided the music. Their work here was done, as far as I knew.

"We couldn't miss you sticking it to the man," Luke said, his eyes twinkling.

The crowds of students in the bleachers burst into applause as Carrie's show ended. The sound echoed in the oversized space.

"Thank you! Look for my video on YouTube!" Carrie called into the microphone, flushed and beaming. As an afterthought she added, "Go, Bobcats."

"Now's your chance." Flynn elbowed me, grinning. "See you in music class."

"There's a keyboard on that stage with your name on it," Luke said.

"I just . . . I didn't have a lot of time to work on the song," I said, suddenly nervous. Principal Lessa was making announcements and getting ready to dismiss the students. I had just a few seconds left to make the call. Then the moment would be over.

"I wouldn't have given you that music if I didn't think you could rock it," Luke said.

I didn't know why or how he had such confidence in me, but it was the boost I needed. Before my legs could become fully formed blocks of ice, I ran for the keyboard. I sat down, hovering my fingers over the keys.

I can't do it.

I took a deep breath and glanced at Luke. He held my gaze and gave a reassuring nod.

Luke thought I could do it. I wasn't sure *why* he thought that, but he did. And maybe . . . it was the push I needed? Slowly, I stretched my fingers out.

I hit the first note just as a few students began filing out of the room.

They stopped, though. The students who'd been leaving stopped, turned around, and settled back in just as my fingers settled across the keyboard in earnest, now.

I pushed forward, ignoring the curious gazes on me (and in Flynn's case, the desperate hopefulness in her eyes).

> Sometimes I think I'm falling down /
> I wanna cry I'm callin' out / For one
> more try / To feel alive

My fingers stumbled and my voice caught. My whole body felt hot and my throat was tight. *Maybe this was a terrible idea . . .*

Just then, though, the sound of a full band chimed in behind me. *Sunset Curve!* They were playing with me!

Relief flooded through me. Finally, I could let go, knowing I wasn't alone.

> Life is a risk but I will take it /
> Close my eyes and jump / Together I
> think that we can make it / Come on
> let's run and—
>
> —Rise through the night

I wasn't alone. I didn't have my mother, but with the boys onstage, playing with me, I wasn't on my own anymore. I could do this.

But then, as I sang the last line, I realized—it wasn't just that the band was playing alongside me. Luke was singing with me, too. They *all* were. I glanced out at the audience to confirm what I already knew was true—*they could see the band! Onstage with me!*

This time, the *how* didn't matter. *We were doing this.* I jumped up, grabbing the mic and owning the stage. Reggie took over at the keyboard as Luke and I continued to sing, together.

> Rise through the night, you and I /
> We will fight to shine together /
> Bright forever

The song ended, and the band disappeared just as

quickly as they had appeared when it started. I stood there, breathless, heart fluttering in my throat.

Then the gym *exploded* in a chorus of applause and wild cheering. All those eyes that were trained on me were smiling, encouraging me, telling me they believed in me.

Us. They believed in *us.* Because it hadn't been me alone up there, of course. Sunset Curve had been right beside me the whole time. Even if I was the only one who could see them.

"Hey," someone called from the bleachers. "Where'd the rest of the band go?"

9

Julie

"Seriously . . . where'd the band go?"

It had been just minutes since my—*our*—set ended,
but it felt like hours to me, glued to the stage, blinded by
the spotlight, and totally thrown by what had just happened during my performance. Never mind how to begin
explaining it to the rest of the school, who were all staring
at me like I'd sprouted an extra head that also happened
to be the head of Harry Styles.

Sunset Curve was here. Visible. *To everyone.*

And then they weren't.

The room was foggy, humid, with the tension of one
collectively held breath. Front and center, Carrie and her
Dirty Candi bandmates glared at me, curious and obviously hating themselves for it.

"That . . . is an interesting question . . . that deserves a response," I hedged.

"Wait," one of Carrie's bandmates chimed in, "were those *holograms*?"

Carrie shot her a *zip it* look, but I could have swept her up and kissed her. "Yes!" I blurted. "Yes, they were! I . . . plugged into the ceiling projector before the show. I'd explain, but it involves algorithms and science stuff." Hopefully, that'd be enough to put off any more questions.

Along the far wall, I could see the boys having what looked like a heated rehash of our little performance. Thankfully, they were for sure invisible to everyone else again now. But how was I going to get out of this?

Saved by the bell. Principal Lessa stepped up to the microphone. "Okay, show's over," she said, her voice ringing with authority. "Please head to your next class."

And I wanted to do just that, but before I could, Mrs. Harrison made her way over to me. *Time to face the music* (no pun intended).

I started stammering before she could open her mouth. "Mrs. Harrison, I know I shouldn't have done that without asking, but I needed to show that I belong here."

She gave me a soft half smile. "As amazing as that was, your spot has already been filled by another student. My hands are tied."

My heart sank. Until I heard Principal Lessa's voice. "Mine aren't."

I turned to face her, hope flooding me. *She* gave me a full, bright smile. "As much as I don't approve of your stunt, I'm not going down as the principal who kicked Julie Molina out of our music program, especially not after that performance."

"Thank you!" I shouted, literally jumping up and down with excitement.

"But when you win your Grammy one day, I want to be thanked," she finished. I nodded, still stunned.

Principal Lessa and Mrs. Harrison moved off, leaving me standing right in front of Flynn. I grabbed her in an epic hug . . . but she only gave me a half-hearted one back.

"You okay?" I asked, pulling away.

She shrugged. "I'm great." It was not the shrug of a Flynn who was "great." "When did you start playing with a hologram band?"

Oh. "Um . . . it was just the one song; we're not a band. I mean, *they're* a band. And holograms. Definitely holograms."

"Yeah," Flynn said slowly. "I saw that. And why have you been keeping those cute boys a secret?"

Excellent question, Flynn. I wished I could tell her the truth. Maybe I could?

After all, she was my best friend. We told each other everything.

"Okay, well . . ." I started. "There's an explanation for that, but it's kinda crazy."

"I'm all about crazy. Let's hear it."

"Okay, they're . . ." I couldn't do it. I couldn't look my best friend in the eye and use the word *ghost*. "From Sweden," I said, panicked. "Turns out that in addition to having great meatballs, they're also great at music. They play there, I stream them here. Anyway, who's pumped that I'm back in the music program?" I glanced at her. *Is she buying this?*

Flynn raised a doubtful eyebrow. "Julie, are you lying to me?"

I bit my lip. What was I supposed to do, say, *Okay, yes, I am lying*? And then what? The truth would just not work. "Flynn . . ." I said, struggling, "I'm sorry." It was the best I could do.

It wasn't enough. Not remotely. Flynn shook her head, totally crushed. "'I'm sorry?' That's all you got?"

She was right to be furious. I would've been, if I were her. But in that moment, I just couldn't do it. I couldn't bring myself to open up.

She turned and ran.

I called after her. "Come on, Flynn—wait!" But it was pointless. She was already gone.

10

Reggie

"You guys gotta stop doing this!"

It was Julie, who'd just come around a corner in the hallway to find herself face-to-face with us. We'd been waiting to talk to her since that crazy performance in the auditorium.

(Well, face to *some* of our faces, since we'd arranged ourselves in a little pyramid while we waited, like a musical pep squad or something. Hey, us ghosts have to pass the time somehow!)

I scrambled down from the formation when I saw her, holding up my hand. "Whoa, this one's on you. We were already here. Well, we were over there, but then we came over here." *As long as we're being specific.*

Alex rolled his eyes, and I shrugged.

"Are we not gonna talk about what just happened?" Luke asked.

Julie made a face at him. "Yeah, the whole school just saw you. It's freaking me out!"

"It's freaking me out, too," Alex said. "Why can *you* see us? And why can *everyone* see us when we play music with you? It doesn't make any sense."

"While we're asking questions," I added, "why can my clothes be made of air, but I'm still getting wedgies?"

The wedgie question was maybe not super relevant to the conversation, but it was driving me *crazy*. Some of us were freaked out, yeah. But some of us had a few other things on our mind, too.

Luke gave me a look and waved me off. "The important thing is, we rocked that," he said to Julie. "They were loving you."

"They were loving *us*," she said, smiling. I realized how few times we'd seen her smile since we first met. Her eyes sparkled and her cheeks were flushed and she looked . . . well . . . *happy*.

And also confused. Which, no judgment, so was I. (Not to mention the whole situation with the wedgies.) But it was nice to see a lighter side of Julie for once.

"That was a great song, Luke," she said. "Thank you."

"By the way, did you guys *see* those cheerleaders looking at me? Man, I miss high school," I chimed in, wistful.

Being in a band was *major* social currency for your average high school boy, dead or not.

"I'm so confused, though," Alex said. "The afterlife should come with instructions. A quick-start guide. Something!"

"Well, luckily, everyone believed you guys were holograms," Julie said. "And I got back into the music program."

Strangely, that happy expression from just before had vanished, at exactly the moment I would've expected to be its biggest. This was supposed to be great news.

"Then . . . why do you look so bummed?" I asked. Alex nodded in agreement.

"Yeah," Luke said. "You're making *this* face." He demonstrated, pouting and squeezing his eyes shut. (It was perfect, if I'm being honest.)

"That is *not* my face," Julie said. "Things just got weird with Flynn. She wanted to know who you guys were and I couldn't say." She sighed.

"Sweet! The girls are already asking about us," I said, pumping my fist. I was going for a laugh, but I guess Julie wasn't in the mood. *Okay, okay. I can quit joking around. For a* minute, *anyway.*

"Stop," Julie protested. "This is serious. I can't tell her for the same reason I can't tell my dad. She'll think I've gone off the deep end." She shook her head. "I gotta get to class."

With one last inscrutable glance, she rushed off.

"Later, Julie!" I called after her. Then . . .

Serious minute over. "And tell those cheerleaders I'm single!" I added, trying to lighten the mood.

"And that he's dead!" Alex put in, grinning.

"No, leave that part out!"

We were still laughing as she vanished down the hall.

But as soon as we poofed back to the garage, Alex went from laughing to pacing. I guess the high from performing had worn off, and all the freaked-out-ness of being dead came rushing back in its place. (I'm always telling that dude he needs to chillax. But he never listens.) He was probably going to wear a hole in the floor of the studio from all the walking back and forth, but it was like he couldn't stop.

"I think he's practicing his model strut," I whispered to Luke.

"He's so nervous, he almost makes me nervous," Luke said.

Alex stopped pacing and turned to face them. "You guys know I don't handle change well. Death? That was a change. Then we're ghosts, another change. Oh—and now people can see us when we play with Julie! *Big freaking change!*"

Luke nodded, but I could tell from his eyes that he thought Alex was overreacting a little "It's a *good* change," he said. "With Julie we can be onstage again and be the band we never got to be. Come on, you gotta be down with that."

"Sure, who wouldn't be?" Alex agreed. "It's way better than being just, like, straight-up dead. But I still have questions. I want to know *why*."

"Forget why," Luke said. "I say we officially invite Julie to join Sunset Curve."

"Totally! A new lead singer would make this band legendary," I said. I mean, since we couldn't exactly cash in on the fact that we were ghosts, we needed another way to build some buzz.

"Hey—*I'm* our lead singer," Luke said, offended.

"That girl has the voice of an angel and can make us visible," I pointed out. "Without her, we're just elevator music."

I thought I had made a good point, but Alex immediately went back to pacing.

"And we're on the runway again," Luke quipped.

"Sorry, guys," Alex offered. "I just—need to go clear my head." He reached out to grab the doorknob and it passed right through his hand.

"Just poof out like a normal ghost," I suggested, rolling my eyes. So far, that was the best perk of being dead. But I guess Alex didn't agree.

"Don't tell me how to ghost!" he shouted . . . just before he poofed out.

I looked over at Luke with a sigh. "That guy really needs to relax."

11

Alex

I appeared again right on Hollywood Boulevard, in the middle of the crush of tourists and people dressed up as different movie characters. Two guys in full Ghostbusting gear were walking toward me and I froze. I was ninety percent sure they were in costume, but what if I was about to be . . . busted?

They passed by without noticing me, just like everyone else. I was in the middle of a huge sigh of relief when out of nowhere, I was sideswiped by a skateboarder! He slammed directly into me, knocking me over.

I hit the ground as the skater recovered, kicking his board upright and grabbing it. "Aw, man . . . you dinged my board," he said, inspecting it.

I got to my feet as quickly as I could, indignant. "I

dinged your board? You ran me over! You're lucky I'm—"
I stopped, as my brain caught up to the moment. "Wait,
you ran me over." I looked at him. "You're a ghost, too?"

He gave a sheepish nod. "Ever since I learned the hard
way that skating in traffic is bad." He shrugged. "Sorry I
smashed into you. I thought you were a Lifer and I'd pass
right through you."

"A *Lifer*?" Being dead was hard enough without having
to worry about learning new vocabulary words.

"That's what we call people who are living." He tilted
his head. "You're new to the whole ghost thing, aren't you?"

I flushed. "Is it that obvious?"

He smiled. "Totally. I'm Willie."

He pulled off his helmet, shaking out his hair.

His brown eyes were friendly.

His silky straight, shoulder-length hair shone as it
swayed in the sunlight.

Were we . . . having a moment?

Willie looked at me.

Oh, right. I'd gotten totally lost in my own head.
"Alex," I said finally.

"So what brings you to Hollywood?" Willie asked.
"Picture with Fake Spider-Man?"

I shook my head. "I was having a minor afterlife crisis,
so I was clearing my head. That is, until you scrambled it."

Willie laughed, showing even white teeth. "I totally
pancaked you." When I gave him a stern look, he

amended with, "I mean, I'm sorry. So, minor afterlife crisis, huh?"

I decided to level with him. What did I have to lose by being honest? "Yeah, I just keep freaking out wondering why we're here. Shouldn't we have gone to heaven or something?"

"Who's 'we'?" Willie asked.

"Me and my bandmates. We all died."

"That's tragic, bro. You guys in some kind of accident?"

"You could say that," I hedged. "We ate some bad hot dogs."

"Oh, weirdly, that's what happened to Mozart," Willie said, grinning.

"That's actually comforting," I said. "Can I ask you a few more questions?"

"That kind of your thing, isn't it?" Willie asked. "It's funny. You thought you'd get answers when you died. Now you just have more questions."

"Yeah, hilarious," I said, flat.

"So what caused this crisis, specifically?"

"Julie. She's the girl who discovered us. Or brought us back. I don't even really understand what exactly happened. And did I mention she can see us? Are you understanding my whole freaking-out thing now?"

Willie's forehead crinkled in surprise. "A Lifer can *see* you?

I nodded. "It gets even crazier. This morning when

we played music with her, we became visible to everyone at her school."

Now Willie ran a hand through his hair, pulling it back from his face. "Whoa. I've never heard of that before. Maybe this Julie is connected to your unfinished business."

"Mmm-hmm," I said. "I would totally agree with you . . . if I had any idea what you were talking about."

"Having unfinished business is why people become ghosts when they die. There's still something they need to accomplish. And once they complete it, they can cross over."

That was a new theory. So this situation the guys and I were in was . . . temporary? Possibly? "So how do we figure out what our unfinished business is?"

Willie looked down for a minute. "I don't know. Some ghosts never do. I haven't." At this, he brightened. "But I'm not really worried about it, because being a ghost lets me do my favorite thing: skate anywhere I want without getting busted. When I'm not skating here or at the beach, I'm skating in Justin Bieber's empty pool."

I had to admit, that didn't sound terrible. Except . . . "I'm sorry, who?"

Willie laughed. "You seriously have a lot to catch up on. Check ya later, Hot Dog." He gave me a little hip check to show he was teasing.

"Not a big fan of the nickname. That's how I died," I

reminded him, even though I knew it was just a joke. He bent over and grabbed his board, getting ready to leave.

"Wait, how can I see you again?" I asked. "You know, so you can help me with my ghost questions."

"I'm around. Come find me." He gave me a small smile. "Even if you don't have questions." And just like that, he poofed away.

Even if you don't have questions. Hmm.

I liked the sound of that.

12

Julie

When I got home from school, Dad was at the kitchen table drinking from one of Mom's many old dahlia mugs, surrounded by enough piles of papers to qualify the scene as a fire hazard. "What is all this?" I asked.

"Oh, good, you're home," he said, looking a little frantic. "It's a bunch of info on other schools with music programs and some private lesson stuff. It may look like a mess, but your dad's on top of it . . ." As he said that, one pile toppled completely over, snaking sheets of paper across the floor.

I moved to help Dad pick up everything. "Then good thing for you I got back into the music program at my school," I reassured him.

His eyes lit up. "Please tell me you're not joking." He leaped up and pulled me into a hug so tight I could barely breathe. "I'm so happy!"

"Me too," I said, resting my cheek against his shoulder.

After helping my dad clean up the papers that had fallen (which, by the way, took about a thousand hours), I headed to the studio to see the guys. Reggie and Luke were on the couch with their guitars, fine-tuning something. As I walked into the space, I heard a huge power chord echo out.

"Guys, you aren't supposed to be out here playing alone," I reminded them.

"We're not alone." Reggie motioned from himself to Luke at his side. "We always have each other."

"We had the volume at level one," Luke said.

"But we rocked it at level *ten*!" Reggie said, enthusiastic. "Want us to play it again?"

I gave him my best *not-amused* look.

"I don't think she does," Luke said, correctly reading my expression. He went on. "We've actually been waiting for you to get home. We have some pretty major news. We had a band meeting earlier and . . ." He paused dramatically. "Brace yourself, this is *big*. We'd like you to join Sunset Curve. And no, you're not dreaming."

I was still thinking about how weird things had been at school today. I was too distracted to give Luke the reaction he was counting on. "Oh."

Luke and Reggie exchanged a glance. "That's it? *Oh?*"

Luke asked. "That's what you say when someone gives you socks for your birthday, not when you get invited to join the most epic band ever."

His feelings were hurt. "I'm sorry," I said, trying to sound it. "I'm honored, but I can't think about anything but Flynn right now. She's still mad at me for lying. She won't even answer her phone." She had been sending me straight to voice mail every time I'd called.

"Man, you're in a tough spot," Luke said, sympathetic. "So, you gonna join the band?"

So much for sympathetic. "Read the room, dude," I said.

"Come on," Luke pleaded. "We need you. And you need us. Because you need *music*. We found this poem you wrote. And Reggie and I were working on this melody that would be *perfect* for it." He held up a piece of paper with my handwriting on it.

"Where'd you get that?" I demanded.

"Uh . . . not in your dream box," he stammered.

"You went through my stuff?" My face got hot with anger. "What happened to boundaries?"

Luke stood up. "You need to accept that you're annoyingly talented. I mean, listen to this." He pulled the paper closer to his face and began to sing—my words to Sunset Curve's melody.

And if somebody hurts you / I'm gonna get hurt, too / That's just how we work,

yeah, that's just how we work/
My life, my life would be real low, zero,
flying solo without you

He looked at me, his gaze piercing. "That's a great hook."

But not even the emotion in his eyes could pull me back. "I wrote that about Flynn when she was helping me with all my mom stuff." I thought back to that time, how scary it was, how lonely and afraid I felt.

Lonely, but not *alone.* Never alone. Because Flynn was by my side through it all.

A lump grew in my throat, but I felt motivated. I knew what I had to do. I looked at Luke. "I've gotta go."

"What about the band?" he asked.

"I almost forgot," I said. He perked up, curious. But I wasn't talking about the band. "Stay out of my room while I'm out!"

I stormed off, but not too quickly to hear Luke's reply. "We will, if you join our band!"

I was on my way to find Flynn, but the thing was . . . she happened to find me first. When I came out of the garage, she was coming up our front walk, carrying a giant tote bag. "Flynn!" I was so happy to see her.

Judging solely by her expression, the feeling was anything but mutual. "I've been looking everywhere for you,"

I said, just plowing ahead despite the total lack of response she was giving.

"Not everywhere," she said, dry, "'cause here I am."

Right. "And . . . I've been texting you. You could've at least texted me back."

She widened her eyes in frustration. "I sent you that poop emoji. I think it said everything."

I tried not to roll my eyes. "Come on, Flynn. I want to tell you how sorry I am. You mean everything to me, and there's no way I would've made it through the last year if it wasn't for you."

She put a hand on her hip. "Yet it was three strangers who got you back into music." She shook her head. "I don't need someone in my life who lies and keeps thing from me. Goodbye, Julie."

She stomped past me. *What do I do?* She was leaving! This was my last chance to come clean!

Without thinking, I blurted: "They're ghosts!"

Flynn stopped in her tracks. Slowly, she turned to face me. "*What?*"

"The guys in my band. They're not holograms. They're ghosts. And when we play together, everyone can see them." It sounded bonkers, saying it out loud. Heck, it sounded bonkers inside my head. But I had to trust that Flynn would trust *me.*

"What do you mean, ghosts? Like the kind that rattle chains and go *Boooooo*?"

"No. And I'm pretty sure that's just a hurtful ghost stereotype. These guys are just regular, normal dead dudes." I reconsidered. "Well, Reggie is a little questionable."

I looked over at Flynn again to see how she was taking this all.

Apparently, she was taking it by texting.

"Who are you texting?"

"Your dad," she said. "He told me to tell him if I was worried about you and, uh . . . I'm worried. You're seeing things."

I sighed. "All right. You wanna be difficult? Meet me down in my mom's studio in half an hour and I'll prove it to you."

Flynn stared at me, steady.

"Please don't text my dad," I added.

Now it was Flynn's turn to sigh. "You have thirty minutes."

I smiled . . . until my gaze caught a carton of eggs peeking out of Flynn's tote. "Eggs?" I asked, suspicious. "Why did you bring eggs?"

Flynn blinked, looking nervous. "Oh, I grabbed those by mistake." Her eyes were wide, flitting around. "It's not like I was going to throw them at your bedroom window or anything!"

Ha. Well, just another crisis we managed to sidestep. "Thirty minutes," I told her.

13

Flynn

Okay, okay, so I would never have *actually* egged Julie's house. (Probably.)

But I wasn't bluffing when I said I was going to text her dad. That stuff Julie was saying about ghosts? That was nuts. And if Julie was being a little bit cuckoo, maybe she *did* need to talk to someone about it. There was no shame in that. After her mother died, she'd seen a psychologist, who helped her learn some coping strategies. I told her dad that if I ever thought she needed to go back for a few more sessions, I'd let him know. Because that's what friends do for each other.

But first, I had to see what she had in store for me, here in her mother's studio.

She'd left the door open, but I knocked, just so she knew I was coming in.

I walked inside to see Julie sitting at the keyboard all by herself. The room itself felt so much like the spirit of Mrs. Molina, I had to admit. So the fact that Julie was in here at the keyboard already told me how far she'd come since losing her mother.

Then Julie turned like she was about to say something—except, not to me. She craned her head like she was looking at someone else. Which would have been fine . . . except there was *no one else* in the room.

"All right, guys, here we go!" she called. Then she looked at me. "Could you stand over there?" She waved to one corner. "Reggie wants to be able to rock out, and he feels weird about walking through you."

Whoo, boy. "When you create a world, you really live in it," I marveled.

"Just get over there." She shooed me. I moved.

"You'll notice I don't have any equipment that would produce a hologram. Feel free to look around," she suggested.

I humored her and took a quick look right and left.

"The guys put a poem I wrote about you to music."

A poem she wrote about me. I'll admit, that one got me. "Aw, I wish I didn't have to talk to your dad after this," I said, meaning it. It really was a shame that my best friend had finally cracked.

"It's called 'Flying Solo,' and I hope you like it."

I gave the best grin I could muster, nervous for what

was about to happen. But she was grinning back at me like she just couldn't wait to blow my mind.

She launched into the opening notes of her song.

> If I leave you on a bad note /
> Leave you on a sad note / Guess
> that means I'm buying lunch that day

I had to laugh. *Darn straight.*

I was still laughing when suddenly, out of nowhere, a flash of light exploded and the three boys from the hologram band appeared next to Julie, with their instruments.

Suddenly, all four of them were singing together, just like they had in school yesterday.

> My life, my life would be real low,
> zero, flying solo without you

My jaw dropped open. These guys *definitely* weren't holograms. And they were singing to me. One moved closer to me, serenading me. I reached out . . . *and my hand passed right through him!*

He laughed. "Weird, right?"

Oh. My. God.

Julie was telling the truth!

They kept playing as I leaped up and grabbed Julie by the shoulders. "They're *ghosts*!" *Ghosts!* How was that even possible? I had so many questions.

The blond one—Alex, that was what Julie had called

him—tapped at his drums while he grinned at me. "We prefer musician spirits."

Still strumming his guitar, Luke sidled up to Julie, playful. "So, does this mean you'll be joining our band?"

I shot him a look. "I think you guys are joining *her* band."

Julie flashed the biggest smile I'd seen on her face in ages. "I'm gonna go with what she said." She hummed a few more bars of the song—*our* song. Then she looked at me. "Still want to talk to my dad?"

I rested my elbow on her shoulder, relieved that the truth was out and there were no more secrets between Julie and me. "Nah," I laughed. "I'm good."

14

Julie

Since playing at the spirit rally and officially agreeing to join Sunset Curve after our performance for Flynn, it was like a switch had been flipped. Suddenly, I was feeling like my old self again: confident, outgoing, and even—yes!—*happy* at school. I practically strutted down the halls singing, breaking out my own compositions whenever the spirit moved me. Just this morning, I'd jotted down some new lyrics:

> I got the music, back inside of me /
> Every melody and chord /
> Can't stop the music / Back inside
> my soul / And it's stronger than before

Not only stronger than before—stronger than *ever*. For the past year, I'd walked the halls of school like *I* was practically a ghost. But not anymore. Now I danced down the halls—and all my friends joined in.

Sometimes, I did get a little bit carried away.

"Hey!"

Like now—I'd been so caught up in the drumming in my head, I'd grabbed a pair of drumsticks from another guy in the hall just to bang out a rhythm against my locker. Now he wanted them back.

"Are you done?" He glared, impatient. "I need my sticks."

Sheepishly, I handed them over and dug the stuff for my next class out of my locker. Once I closed the door, I found Flynn looking at me, grinning.

"What's up?" I asked.

"Nothing, it's just nice to see you back to being your weirdo self," she said.

"Thanks?" I joked, even though I knew she meant it as a legit compliment.

"So, how's the band?" she asked. "Still hot? Still talented?" She lowered her voice to a whisper. "Still dead?"

"Amazing," I gushed. "Luke and I had so much fun writing this weekend. Come on, you have to hear these." I pulled her into the music room, which was blissfully empty at this hour.

"The music was just bursting out of me," I told her as we closed the door to the room. "It was like when I was writing with my mom." I sat down at the piano and began to play for her.

"Definite Gaga vibes," Flynn said, nodding along approvingly.

"Thanks. And I think we have an anthem in this one. It's something my mom and I were working on . . ." My eyes welled up, and I took a breath to compose myself. "Anyway, Luke and I finished it. Check it out." I played a few bars.

I paused when I realized Flynn's eyes were welling up, too. "That's . . . beautiful." Then she smiled at me knowingly. "My girl's got a crush."

"What?" My cheeks flamed with embarrassment. "Um, no way. Luke's a ghost, remember?"

"Luke's a *cute* ghost," she corrected me.

I couldn't help it, I melted, the warmth from my cheeks enveloping me like a fuzzy blanket. "With a perfect smile," I added.

"Ha! I knew it. Just remember, he's made of air." Flynn wagged a finger at me.

"*Cute* air."

"Obviously, you two have a connection. Just don't get hurt, okay? Especially because everyone's been asking when your band is going to play again."

That was news to me. "Play again? But we don't have anything planned. Luke and I have just been focused on writing songs."

"Lucky for you, your marketing team is way ahead of you."

"I don't have a marketing team."

"Yeah, you do," Flynn insisted. She pointed at herself. "And surprise—you're playing the dance tonight that I'm going to DJ! See?" She pulled out a flyer from her pocket and unfolded it so that I could read:

Julie and her Hologram Band—tonight at the dance!

"I posted it all over social media," she said, proud. "You have an excellent marketing team."

"What?" This was too much. Too fast. "This is in front of the whole school."

Never gonna happen.

Flynn saw the look on my face and giggled. "Sorry, but you already have sixty-eight likes . . ."

Okay, well . . . I guess now I just had to break the news to the guys . . .

"It's not exactly the Sunset strip."

That was Luke's reaction after school when I told the boys about the gig Flynn had lined up for us. He and Reggie were hanging in the studio, but Alex was nowhere to be found. They said he'd been out taking walks, poofing away for some quiet time. They assured me he was fine, just sensitive—I hoped that was all it was.

"And we're not exactly alive," Reggie pointed out. "So maybe you should be happy we have our first official gig together as a band. And at a school dance? Sweet!"

I was super grateful for Reggie's enthusiasm. "I wasn't in love with the idea at first, either," I admitted to them. "But it could be great for us. It's how we build a following, right?"

"Yeah," Reggie agreed. "We need to play wherever we can, whenever we can."

"No, you're right," Luke said, relenting. "We'll rock those kids' faces off. Then we'll start playing clubs . . ."

"Then record a single that'll get a billion streams . . ." I said.

Luke gave me a confused look. "Don't know what that is."

(I kept forgetting that they were totally behind on any pop culture that took place after 1995. Which was a lot.)

"But, hopefully, it leads to us getting a manager and going on tour," he finished.

"Then we release a bunch of hit albums!" I said.

"What are we waiting for?" Luke asked, getting into the spirit of it. "Let's start rehearsing. Except—where's Alex?"

It turned out, no one knew. *Right.* That's *what we were waiting for.*

15

Alex

Willie and I had been hanging out more and more since we first met, and today he wanted to show me one of his favorite places. Willie said you hadn't really lived until you'd skated the floors of the contemporary art museum. I tried to remind Willie that we *couldn't* actually live, right now, what with how we were *ghosts*, but he didn't seem all that hung up on the language.

"I feel like this isn't about the art," I said, standing in front of the museum's closed—and locked—doors. "You just like breaking rules." That was my takeaway.

"Maybe," he said. "You should try it sometime."

I looked at him. "We're going in there, aren't we?"

He smiled and took my hand.

Between both those things, I suddenly didn't care how

many rules we were breaking. I would have followed Willie just about anywhere . . .

Once we were inside, Willie quickly put on his helmet.

"Sick," I said, taking in the big, empty spaces and the concrete floors. The atrium was closed for renovations and there were all kinds of sawhorses and things spread out—a makeshift skate park, for sure.

"And we have the place all to ourselves," Willie said, taking off.

After a while of winding around the sculptures (which, I had to admit made me pretty nervous), he took a break. "Hey, slide that bench over here. I'm gonna try to jump it."

He pointed to something huge and stone. "I can't move that." I shook my head. "I can barely move small things."

Willie laughed. "Trust me. If you concentrate on putting all your energy in your hands, you can move anything. Here, we'll do it together."

Together. I liked the sound of that. Willie grabbed one end of the bench and I tried to grab the other . . . but my hands went straight through it, just like always. "Guess I need to start doing ghost push-ups," I said.

"Just focus," Willie said.

"Yeah, I have a hard time focusing," I admitted. "I was always pretty anxious, and then I died, which did not calm me down."

Gently, Willie took my hand in his. He guided me back to the bench. This time, I imagined my energy like a beam of light, shining straight ahead onto the solid stone of the bench. *Close . . . close . . .*

If the bench did move, it was barely a centimeter. But it was *something*. I felt it. And that was huge.

"Not bad," Willie said, approving. "We'll keep working on it. You'll see—you'll get it in no time."

I hoped he was right.

"Is that why you got into drums?" he went on. "To help you with your anxiety?"

"Pretty much. There's no better way to work out your problems than wailing on some drums."

Willie looked at me like he was thinking something over. "Do you know what makes me feel better?"

Why did I not like the look of that gleam in his eye?

"Yelling in museums." He gave a full-on grin and belted one out. "AHHHHH!"

I looked at him. "Ahh."

"You gotta put your heart into it!" he insisted, grabbing me. He leaned in, so close I could feel his breath when he opened his mouth to scream again. "AHHHH!"

I did it, too. I finally let go. All the stress, all the worry . . . twenty-five years of crying! *"AHHHH!"*

Now we were both screaming. We were laughing, too.

"Feels good, right?" he asked, eyes twinkling.

"Yeah," I said. "It does."

I was talking about the screaming, but I was talking about being here, now, with Willie, too.

16

Julie

We were still rehearsing for the dance when Alex finally poofed back. He said he'd been out on one of his pacing walks, and the guys seemed to take that at face value. I didn't know Alex well enough yet to be able to judge, but I did vow to try to keep a closer eye on him, to make sure he was okay. We filled him in quickly, then it was time to put together our set list.

"Remind me later to show you some Sunset Curve songs we want to do with you," Luke said.

"Ooh, show me now," I said, wagging an eyebrow.

Luke picked up his notebook and flipped to a dog-eared page. "This one's got a great riff." He picked up his guitar to show me.

Oh, a classic. "So you want to sample?" I asked.

"What do you mean? What's sample?" Luke asked, confused.

"Sample someone else's song," I explained. "Me and my mom used to sing that at the top of our lungs in the car. It's a classic Trevor Wilson song."

Now Luke looked *totally* lost. "No, it's a classic *our* song."

"Pure Sunset Curve," Reggie agreed. "I've never heard of Trevor Wilson."

"Maybe you're mixing it up with another song?" Alex suggested.

"I don't mix up songs," I insisted. "Trust me, I used to be best friends with his daughter and hang out at their house all the time. I know the song. Here—I'll prove it." I pulled out my laptop, searching Google while I talked. A few taps on the keyboard and there it was. I turned the screen around to show them.

"Trevor Wilson. His first album had a ton of hits. But his later stuff was never as good."

Luke's eyes flew open. "That's Bobby!"

"Seriously? I *just* told you his name is Trevor." The guys were being so insistent; it was weird.

"Well, he must have changed it because that's definitely Bobby," Alex put in. "He was our rhythm guitarist."

I couldn't help but laugh. "*Trevor Wilson* was in your band?" It was just hard to put it together—that major star and these . . . well, *ghosts,* living in my mother's music studio.

Reggie looked horrified at the image on the screen. "I can't get over how old he looks!"

Alex made a face. "Yeah . . . he looks like a substitute teacher."

Luke looked at me, suspicious. "What were his other hits?"

I thought about it. "'Get Lost.'"

"Yeah," Luke said, taking his guitar off. "I wrote that."

"'Long Weekend'?" I tried.

"Luke wrote that, too!" Reggie said.

"'Crooked Teeth'?" I almost didn't want to ask.

"And that!" Alex confirmed. "It was about Reggie."

"I thought it was about *you*!" Reggie protested. "I don't like that song anymore."

"Wait," I said, pressing my hands to my temples. "This is freaking me out. Trevor's songs are kind of a big deal to me. He introduced me to rock." If Trevor's biggest hits were actually taken from his time with Sunset Curve . . . what did that mean?

Alex stated the obvious. "No, he didn't. *Luke* introduced you to rock."

I glanced at Luke. "All this time, I was hoping you guys were connecting me to my mom. But instead, you're connecting me to *Carrie's dad*? Of all people, why the one girl who has it out for me?" I couldn't believe it. This would have been upsetting even *without* the whole confusing Carrie part of it.

Alex shook his head, obviously as thrown as I was—as we all were. "Add it to our list of questions. Bobby was our friend. He would've never done something like that."

"But *Trevor* did," Reggie said.

My mind raced. "Back when Carrie and I were friends, the three of us would talk music all the time. He never mentioned you guys." *Which meant . . .*

"Unbelievable," Luke said, disgusted. "He took all the credit, and no one knows it but us." He pulled one of the darts from the dartboard hanging in the corner of the studio.

"And he's rich," I said. "He has his own helicopter."

Thwack. One of the darts sailed straight into the target of the dartboard.

"We live in a garage!" Alex protested.

I resisted the urge to point out that technically, they didn't *live* anywhere.

"It's not about the money, guys," Luke said.

"It's a *little* bit about the money, though!" Reggie said. "He could've shared it with our families. Maybe then my parents' house wouldn't have been turned into a bike shack."

"What he did was steal our legacy," Luke said. He turned to me. "Where does he live?"

"Above the beach in Malibu."

"Let's go teach him a lesson," Luke said.

There were a million reasons why this was a terrible idea—for one, we had to rehearse for the dance—but before I could even get one of them out, the boys had poofed from the garage, leaving me all alone to think about Trevor Wilson.

And how he was a liar and a thief.

In 1995, Sunset Curve was on their way to stardom . . . until a couple of bad street hot dogs ended their rock band dreams—and their lives.

ROCK

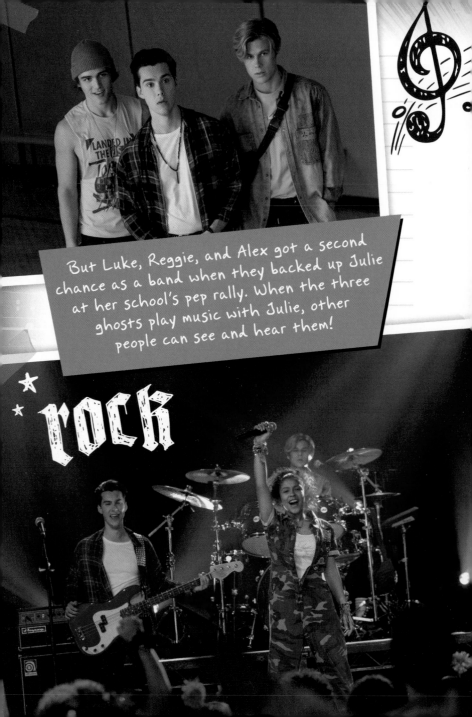

But Luke, Reggie, and Alex got a second chance as a band when they backed up Julie at her school's pep rally. When the three ghosts play music with Julie, other people can see and hear them!

rock

Don't look down / 'Cause we're still
rising / Up right now

And even if w
We'll still fly
like we'll live
it like it's now

It's now or n

Julie convinces everyone that the guys are a
hologram band from Sweden—except for her
best friend. Flynn is hurt that Julie is keeping
secrets, but once she learns that the band
members are ghosts, Flynn becomes Julie and
the Phantoms' biggest fan!

But being a band isn't always easy. After Luke, Reggie, and Alex get distracted at Caleb Covington's Hollywood Ghost Club, they end up blowing off their first real gig at Julie's school dance. The guys have to make it up to her **big** time. Luckily, they're able to use their ghostly powers to snag a spot at a local café's open-mic night—and even catch the attention of a music exec.

The band continues to grow their fanbase after another incredible performance in Julie's backyard. And during their set, Luke and Julie share a special moment. Could Julie have a crush on a ghost?

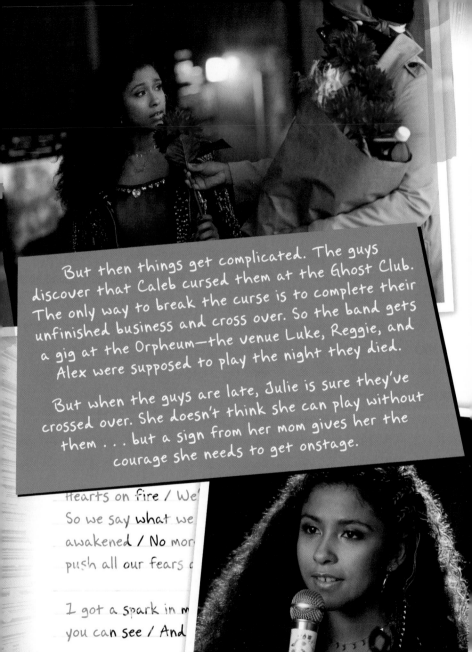

But then things get complicated. The guys discover that Caleb cursed them at the Ghost Club. The only way to break the curse is to complete their unfinished business and cross over. So the band gets a gig at the Orpheum—the venue Luke, Reggie, and Alex were supposed to play the night they died.

But when the guys are late, Julie is sure they've crossed over. She doesn't think she can play without them . . . but a sign from her mom gives her the courage she needs to get onstage.

Hearts on fire / We'
So we say what we
awakened / No mor
push all our fears a

I got a spark in m
you can see / And

Midsong at the Orpheum, the guys finally explode onto the stage. They managed to escape Caleb's clutches and make their way back to Julie. Julie and the Phantoms rock the house one last time before Luke, Reggie, and Alex fade away. But are they really gone?

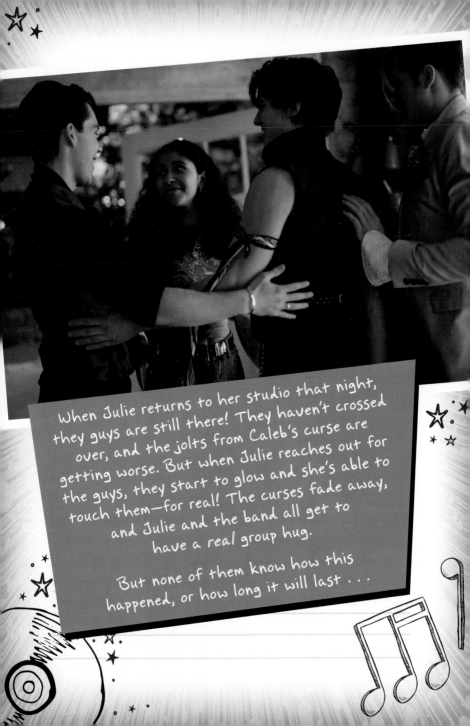

When Julie returns to her studio that night, they guys are still there! They haven't crossed over, and the jolts from Caleb's curse are getting worse. But when Julie reaches out for the guys, they start to glow and she's able to touch them—for real! The curses fade away, and Julie and the band all get to have a *real* group hug.

But none of them know how this happened, or how long it will last . . .

17

Luke

I never really did believe much in karma. After all, I died eating an expired hot dog. Like, what could I possibly have done in a past life to deserve *that*?

But wandering around Trevor's mansion—with its huge open spaces, giant windows overlooking the glittering ocean and a cloudless sky, lined with photos of him hanging out with every major music star of the past two decades (I had to assume) . . .

Well, I hoped karma had a few things in store for him.

"Bobby's house is ridiculous," Alex said. He pointed to the framed albums on the walls. "Have you seen the platinum records?"

I looked at one. "He recorded 'My Name Is Luke,'" I said, incredulous. "*My* name is Luke!"

Then the front door opened and a greasy-haired

middle-aged man in a motorcycle jacket wandered in. He was still wearing his sunglasses. "Hey, Carrie, I'm gonna meditate!" he called out.

"That's him! He wears sunglasses indoors," Reggie said, upset. "I can't stand him!"

I glared at him, watching with fury as he went off to "meditate." "Time for his past to haunt him," I said, menacingly.

———

We were right behind Bobby—*Trevor*—as he made his way up the stairs.

The meditation room turned out to be, like, a yoga studio, with tons of pillows, dim lighting, incense . . . and a little altar covered in candles. That made the haunting easier at least. Trevor lit one right away, making prayer hands and lowering himself onto an ottoman. I grinned. This was going to be fun.

Knowing he couldn't see me (and for once, super pumped about it), I stepped forward and blew out the candle.

He sat cross-legged and placed his hands on his knees. "*Ommmmm*," he chanted. But he only made it halfway through the mantra before I stuck my wet finger in his ear. Oh, no you don't. This was a haunting, after all.

He flinched, making a face and shaking his head like a dog trying to dry off after a rainstorm. Then he settled back in. "*Ommmmm . . .*"

Clearly we had to up our game. Good thing we'd been practicing how to move things. Alex had passed along some tips from his friend Willie's ghost lessons, and it was paying off big-time! We were basically pros now. This time we managed to switch Trevor's New Age whale sounds to some serious electric guitar.

"Carrie?" he asked, finally looking seriously weirded out. *Good.* He stood up to turn off the stereo, which was when we turned the shower in the adjoining bathroom *on.*

He jumped back, then peered around. Reluctantly, he walked into the bathroom, knocking on the door even though we all knew there wasn't anyone there.

(Well, no one *alive*, anyway.)

The shower had steamed up the bathroom mirror. In an inspired moment, I wrote "HI BOBBY" in the condensation.

That did it; Trevor was totally freaked. He darted for the bathroom door—only for us to slam it in his face!

He pounded on the door, his man bun bobbing. "LET ME OUT!" But we were having too much fun for that just yet.

I turned the music back on.

We let him wrestle with the doorknob for a few seconds, loving the panic rising in his eyes. When Alex finally let the door open, he raced out.

"Carrie! I'm gonna go see my therapist!"

The next thing we knew, he was taking off in his own

private helicopter. *Of course he has a private helicopter.* We should've haunted him harder.

Had he paid enough? Not nearly. Not yet. But it was still a good start.

We were still watching him fly off in the distance when Julie found us on the helipad. I guess we should have known she'd show up eventually.

"Did you guys have fun in there?" she asked, obviously annoyed.

"Come on," I said, "you'd do the same if someone stole all your songs."

"But you have *new* songs, with *me*," she reminded us. "The best way to get back at Trevor is for *this* band to do great. And to do great, we need to play dances, then clubs . . ."

"Then tour, I know." I sighed. I *did* know. And I should have known better than to run off on my own personal revenge scheme when Julie was counting on us. Because we were counting on her, too. And, the truth was, she was becoming important to me. I hated to let her down.

"I have to go start setting up, but I'll see you guys at the school. We go on at nine. Please don't be late," she said, her eyes on me, imploring. "A lot of people are gonna be there."

"We got it," I promised her. "Don't worry."

After Julie left, though, Alex and Reggie and I agreed—dumb, personal revenge or not—we were *glad* we'd scared Bobby. And the truth was, we wanted to do it again. We wanted to do it *more*. Which meant that we had more to learn.

"Hey, Alex, you think Willie might have a few more tricks up his sleeve?" I asked.

Sure, we had the ghostly basics down. But, now, I wanted to kick it up a notch. And I had a feeling I wasn't the only one.

Alex grinned and nodded.

"Well," I said, "maybe we should swing by and talk to him before it's time to meet Julie."

Maybe more tricks are just what we need.

18

Alex

We found Willie in the park, skating, of course. I was happy to introduce my friends to him—it was kind of cool to be the only one of the three of us to have a connection beyond just our band. And Willie showed the guys how to move heavier things and stuff, just like he taught me. But Luke wanted to go bigger. He wanted to learn how to talk to Lifers. We explained what we needed.

"Sorry," Willie said, "talking to Lifers is even out of my league." He paused for a minute, thoughtful. "But there is one ghost who might be able to help. He's kind of a big deal."

The next thing we knew, we'd poofed to a glamorous old-school Hollywood hotel—the kind that you'd see in black-and-white movies. Willie led us up the stairs into a grand lobby, with a giant crystal chandelier overhead and a shiny marble-tiled floor.

"So this is where your hotshot ghost lives, huh?" Luke asked, impressed by the place. "Word."

"We've passed by this hotel a million times, but I never knew this was here," I said. Leave it to Willie to find some secret, back-alley section of the place to use as a hangout.

"This area's been sealed off for decades," Willie explained. "If you weren't invited, you wouldn't even know it exists. I'm just gonna go make sure everything's cool. Be right back."

Reggie wandered back and forth, looking at the posters and old signs that were hanging. "Hollywood Ghost Club?" he read. "This place is creepy."

"Yeah, well—so are we." I felt a little defensive, since this was Willie's place and everything. Sort of.

"I don't know about this," Reggie shot back.

"Hey, if you get scared, you can hide behind me," I said. I smiled to show I was mostly kidding. "I'll be hiding behind Luke."

"Grow up, you two," Luke said impatiently. "We're gonna do whatever it takes to get back at Bobby. He needs to pay for ripping us off."

Abruptly, Willie poofed back into the lobby. "We're good," he said. He began to lead us toward the grand staircase in the center of the room.

"Just so you know," I told him, "we only have, like, an hour before we've got the gig with Julie."

"No worries, follow me." He winked. "Hope you guys are ready for this."

As we walked down the staircase, my jaw dropped. I didn't think that was a thing that literally happened, but I guess I was wrong. Willie led us to a secret ballroom that was everything I'd imagined old Hollywood to be. I'd never seen a place as fancy as this in real life.

And it was filled with Lifers.

They were dressed like it was an awards show, all in deep black or brilliant white, with jewels shining everywhere. Jazzy music played in the background.

"Wow . . ." Reggie breathed, totally blown away.

"I think we're a little underdressed," Luke joked. Immediately, out of habit, all three of us went to tuck our shirts in and smooth down our collars.

"This is a very exclusive crowd," Willie went on. "Everyone here paid a lot to get a peek at the afterlife."

Reggie shook his head. "Wait. *They can see us here?* I always knew rich people did weird stuff like this."

Like this? *Really?* I didn't say it.

A ghost maître d' poofed out of thin air (I mean, technically, I guess that's what all poofing was—but this felt especially abrupt). He wore a tuxedo and looked extremely fancy. That seemed like the theme in this place. He led us to a table with a little sign on it: RESERVED. WILLIAM, PARTY OF FOUR.

I turned to thank him as I sat down . . . but he'd already vanished.

Luke was edgy, jiggling in his seat and scanning the room. "So how do we stay visible *outside* this club, too, so we can confront our old bandmate?"

"Oh, no one here has the power to do that," Willie said.

Luke made a face like he was going to ask a question— *How can all the Lifers* in here *see us, then?* I wanted to ask it myself—but before he could say anything, the house lights dimmed and the audience snapped to attention. The room buzzed with anticipation.

"But here comes the ghost who does," Willie whispered.

An announcer's voice boomed through the space. "*Ladies and gentlemen, back from the dead by POPULAR DEMAND, the one, the only . . . CALEB COVINGTON!*"

A spotlight cut through the darkness landing on—I guess—Caleb, who floated down toward the stage in a top hat and tails. His eyes were an electric blue and his smile was almost as blinding as the spotlight. Something about him was familiar, but I couldn't quite put my finger on it . . .

As the ghost touched down on the stage, he tipped his hat to the cheers of the crowd. "Did you miss me?" His voice was pure velvet. Judging from the applause, people definitely missed him. He beamed, drinking it in. "I missed me, too!

"Welcome," he said, spreading his arms wide, "to the party of your dreams! From the Egyptians to the Druids to the person sitting next to you, we've all wondered: Where do we go when the final light is snuffed out?"

A murmur of agreement broke out among the crowd. "Allow me to show you!" Caleb said, spreading his arms wide.

He floated back up as an orchestra began its overture. Bobbing among the audience, he began to sing.

> Let me introduce myself / We got
> some time to kill / Consider me the
> pearly gates to your new favorite thrills

The audience ate him up as he swooped and soared through the crowd. He wavered near our table but took a moment to jokingly hypnotize some of the Lifers in the group. Then he was back, lingering over us, singing promises of a better life . . . er, afterlife, I guess.

> Life is good / On the other side of
> Hollywood / Life is good /
> On the other side of Hollywood /
> So welcome to the brotherhood /
> Where you won't be misunderstood /
> Life is good / On the other side
> of Hollywood
>
> Everything has got a price /

*But happiness is free / Just so happens /
You're in luck / We've got a vacancy*

I glanced at Willie, who was smiling at me, enjoying how blown away the guys and I were by the whole performance, the place, Caleb . . . everything. The music was amazing, Caleb's stage presence was magnetic, and it was completely insane knowing we were sitting at a table, surrounded by people who could see us, just like we could see them. Even though we weren't playing, and we weren't with Julie. A couple at a table nearby waved at us, and Reggie waved back with excitement. Meanwhile, a group of waiters danced around us with platters of decadent food and an array of desserts. People could see us. People could hear us. And in this club . . . we could *eat*?

Oh, I missed eating.

"This is so cool!" Reggie said, echoing my thoughts.

"I knew I recognized that guy!" I said, putting it together. "He was the one who bumped into me outside the Orpheum." It had taken me a minute, I was so blown away by the club, but it was definitely him.

"Isn't he the magician who died doing one of his tricks?" Reggie asked, remembering.

"Yeah . . . I wouldn't bring that up when we meet him," I said.

"So he waves his arms and he can make ghosts visible to Lifers?" Luke asked, trying to understand.

"The guy has skills," Willie said.

"Wait, where'd he go?" Reggie asked, squinting at the now empty stage.

Poof! Caleb appeared right behind us! We all jumped up, startled.

"Found him!" Reggie said.

"Hello, gentlemen. Caleb Covington. Welcome to the Hollywood Ghost Club. Enjoying the show?"

Even Luke was totally thrown. "I can't . . . you were . . ." he stammered. "That performance *ruled.*"

Caleb gave him a knowing smile. "Yes, it did."

Willie stepped forward to introduce us. "This is Alex, Luke, and Reggie."

"Nice to meet you," I said, sounding exactly as awestruck as I was feeling.

"The pleasure is mine," Caleb said. "Nothing warms my heart more than sharing this magic with new friends. Please, sit."

The maître d' pulled up an extra chair, and we settled back at the table.

"Now," Caleb said, "my friend Willie tells me you boys have some magic of your own."

I don't know that I would call what Willie and I had *magic. Or would I?* "Oh, well, we—"

"He means your ghost abilities," Willie said, cutting me off. "You know, how everyone sees you when you play with Julie."

"Right, yeah. That. For sure." *I definitely knew that's what he meant.*

"But we can't—wave our arms and make all this magic happen," Luke put in.

Caleb gave him an understanding look. "I've had some practice. Our gifts are so rare. So special. It's not often I come across other spirits who possess similar . . . talents. It's no surprise we found one another."

"Definitely," Luke said, looking totally mesmerized.

"Forgive me," Caleb said abruptly. "Gotta go pay the bills, if you know what I'm saying. I'll be back later to chat." He flashed us one last dazzling Hollywood smile and left the table.

"I love that dude," Reggie said, sighing as we watched Caleb move off. "Tell me this party's never gonna end."

19

Julie

I mean, they say a watched pot never boils. But staring at my watch over and over again, desperate for the guys to show up at school, was *not* making time pass any slower. *It's 9:15 p.m. Where are they?*

Flynn and her DJ skills were keeping the crowd at the dance happy—for now. But how much time could she buy? I peered at her from my perch backstage, in the wings, hating how hot my face felt, how much more nervous I was getting with each passing minute.

"Is everyone fired up about Julie and the Phantoms?" she called.

Everyone cheered.

"Great!" she said. "Keep that fire—'cause that's later! We're just a little behind schedule." I could hear her struggle to sound cool. "In the meantime, enjoy these *mind-blowing beats*!" She dropped another beat and—thank *god*—the crowd immediately got into it, jumping up and down.

They were *way* more amped up than I was feeling.

Flynn met me backstage. I looked at her. "Julie and the Phantoms?"

She shrugged. "I had some time in French class. You better like it 'cause I already registered it on Twitter, Insta, and Snapchat."

I sighed. "No, I love it. I would just love it more if the actual Phantoms were here."

"Hey."

Flynn and I both turned.

"Nick?" I was so surprised, I completely spazzed out. "Nick! Look, Flynn—Nick's here. It's Nick." *OMG Julie: chill, girl.*

Nick smiled. "Thanks for the introduction."

Flynn wagged an eyebrow at me and slipped away knowingly.

"I didn't know you were coming tonight," I said when it was just Nick and me.

"Wouldn't miss it," he said, making my heart flutter. "The truth is, I couldn't wait to see you play again. Your song's been stuck in my head since I heard you play at the pep rally."

Wow. I swallowed, not knowing what to say to that. Nick and I had been friends for ages—and my crush on him had lasted for almost as long—but ever since Carrie and I fell out, things were weird between us. When your crush's girl-friend is your frenemy, things tend to get awkward.

"Hey, I like your shoes," Nick said, breaking me out of my reverie.

I looked down to my tennies, which I'd decorated with lots of colorful little drawings. It was just something I did when I was bored. "Oh, thanks. I just like to doodle—"

"I can't tell if the crowd is getting restless or bored. Never a good sign." It was Carrie, sidling up to Nick with her fake-sweet smile. She glanced at me like she'd just realized I was there. "Oh hi, Julie." She scanned the space, her gaze landing on the little small projector box I'd stashed on the dais. "What's that?"

"My new hologram projector," I said. "Did a little upgrade." Still had to keep up appearances, after all—*that is, if the band ever actually* makes *an appearance.*

"Huh," Carrie said, her voice deceptively bright. "So simple. I was expecting something a little more sophisticated."

I looked at her. "It's what's on the inside that counts."

She smiled. "Yeah, that's what a lot of people have to tell themselves." She grabbed Nick's arm possessively. "Come on, Nick," she said, leading him away.

"Why can't you just chill?" I heard Nick ask as they wandered off. I was having a rotten night, so far, but knowing he wasn't totally brainwashed by her helped.

"I'm sorry," Carrie sniffed, "but there's something about amateur night that makes me a little queasy."

Yeah, I thought, that slight thrill of Nick standing up to Carrie deflating. I was feeling a little nauseated myself.

———

"I can only stall for so long."

Flynn stood over me backstage in full "moment of truth" mode. I couldn't bring myself to look at her, so I fiddled with my projector—pretending like it even mattered. *Ha.*

"You should just play by yourself. Holograms or no holograms, you'll be amazing."

"You saw me the other day," I protested. "I can't do it without them. They'll be here. They have to."

With a heavy sigh, Flynn returned to her DJ table.

"Issues?"

I looked up. *Nick.* How had he managed to sneak up on me, not once but twice tonight?

"Always," I said, hoping he was buying it. "Machine won't work."

He lifted the cord and began to follow it to the power source. "Oh," I said, "you really don't have to . . ."

"Here's the problem!" he said, bright. He held the cord up. "The plug's not in."

Busted. What now? My shoulders and my spirits sagged. "Thanks," I mustered.

Nick gave me a strange look. "Unless you didn't want it plugged in?"

So busted.

Nick's gaze softened. "Hey, don't let this crowd freak you out. What I saw last time you played was *insane*. You got this."

He didn't get it. But he was *so* sweet.

And he . . . was moving toward the stage.

Oh no! What was he doing?

I watched in terror as Nick signaled for Flynn to stop the music. He grabbed a mic. "Hey, everybody! We fixed the hologram thing! Who wants to see a show?"

The crowd hooted and hollered. My stomach sank. Flynn shot me a panicked look.

"That's more like it," Nick called into the mic. "Now give it up for *Julie and the Phantoms*!"

The crowd went crazy. It was like nothing I'd ever heard before. And it was for *me*.

For me . . . and the Phantoms . . . who had, ironically, totally ghosted me.

This was my worst nightmare. Way more terrifying than the one where you go on an audition and realize you forgot your sheet music *and* you're naked. I walked numbly toward the stage, trying to tune out the expectant faces and the enthusiastic cheers.

I took the mic from Nick, who beamed at me proudly. *You won't be proud of me in another minute.* "Hi," I said, wincing at the nervous squeak in my voice. "Here's the thing. Even though we fixed the machine—thanks, Nick—I can't seem to link up with the guys." I took a breath. "Wi-Fi, am I right?" I waved my phone, but the awkward "joke" just sat in the air like dead fish. "I'm sorry," I finished. "I'm going to have to cancel."

The *boos* came quickly. Almost as quickly as Carrie's response. "Only one way to save this dance. Party at my house!"

Nick shot me a pleading look, but Carrie hooked an arm through his and led him off, with the crowd cheering again, now.

But this time, they were cheering for Carrie.

20

Willie

I loved how excited Alex and his friends were to be party-ing with Caleb at the hotel. It was nice to see him finally have a little moment to appreciate the upsides that being a ghost could have. The dude was wound so tight! It was fun to party and let loose a little. And this club was the place to do it! Glitz and glamour, twinkling chande-liers, and people dressed all fancy. It was like being on a movie set.

Watching Alex so excited and, well . . . practically *alive* again . . .

It was almost enough to make the guilty chatter in the back of my mind go quiet. *Almost.*

"This is one crazy show," Alex said, leaning into me at the table. Around us, Reggie and Luke were dancing and mingling with all the partygoers. "I'm guessing the Lifers are sworn to secrecy or something?"

"Or something," I told him, hating that I had to be a little cagey. "Let's just say Caleb's offered all the ghosts here, with their membership, the opportunity to experience this for eternity, and they happily accepted." *Of course, there was a catch. But I couldn't get into that right now.*

"And all these ghosts just want to party and not cross over?" Alex sounded incredulous.

"Why cross over when they can hang out and do this forever?" I pointed out. "There's a lot to like here."

Caleb returned to the table with Reggie and Luke, so the whole band was together now. "I take it you boys are enjoying yourselves?"

"You'd have to be insane to have a bad time here," Luke said.

"Entertainment is our specialty," Caleb said. Then he got down to business. "So, I understand there's something I can help you with."

"We hope so," Reggie said. "A buddy of ours ripped us off big-time, and we need to make things right."

"Yeah," Luke added. "We need to look him in the eye and make him admit what he did."

"So if you could make him see us, that would be perfect," Alex said.

"Sure," Caleb replied, agreeable. "I can do that. But

we're at a party. Why focus on those who've wronged us when we're among friends? I understand the three of you are talented musicians. I doubt your dream is to 'settle a score.' It must be bigger than that."

I watched as the boys took that in. Caleb was making his point, perfectly. He always did.

"You're like me," he went on. "Born to perform in front of sold-out crowds. What if I were to tell you that with a wave of my hand, you could share the spotlight with me and join my house band?"

I bristled. That wasn't what Caleb and I had discussed before I brought the guys here.

"We already have a band," Luke pointed out.

"Yes," Caleb said. "But when you're done playing, you cease to exist. No bows. No soaking up the applause. No real connection with the audience."

Alex and Reggie looked at Luke, whose face was tight, obviously intrigued.

"Here the audience knows what you are. And more important," Caleb said, "they know how special you are."

I knew, then, that he had them. Because that was what everyone wanted, wasn't it? Living or dead—we wanted to be reassured that we were special. And that others saw that spark within us.

"Playing here could be cool," Luke said, warming to the idea.

"Oh, it's not just here," Caleb said. "We party like this

all over the world. Tonight, Hollywood, tomorrow, Paris. It's all your dreams come true . . . forever." He paused for impact. I could tell from the guys' expression that it was working.

"I'll give you some time to think about it." He stood, ready to leave. "And by the way, make sure to try the sliders," he added as a last thought. "They're to die for."

———

At midnight, the guys were still having the time of their afterlives. Luke and Reggie were tearing it up on the dance floor with twin flappers, literally being swept off their feet. Alex was also on the dance floor, caught up in the crowd.

As the grand clock on the wall struck twelve, Caleb called out, "The haunting hour is upon us!"

The crowd cheered, but Luke stopped dancing and looked at Reggie, panicked. "Twelve? How'd that happen?" He waved his arm at Reggie. "Dude, we lost track of time."

Reggie waved him away. "Not right now, man."

"We were supposed to be at Julie's school at nine!" Luke insisted.

Finally, what Luke was saying seemed to break through Reggie's haze. He pulled away. "Oh, shoot, that's right. Maybe we can still make it. Alex—" he called out, "We forgot—"

"Julie. I know!" Alex shouted, from where he was

dangling in the air of an aerialist's hoop. "This place is some kind of time warp!"

"Poof down here, bro!" Luke yelled to him. "We've gotta get goin'!"

I followed at a distance and saw Caleb poof in to block their exit.

"Gentlemen, what's the rush? The party's just getting started, and you have an eternity, after all."

"You know that girl who can see us? We sorta bailed on her," Alex explained.

"Basically, we're late for a gig." Luke cut to the chase.

"What about my offer?" Caleb asked.

"It's very cool of you, Mr. Covington, but we've got—" Luke started.

"—your own band. I understand. But, boys, if you ever want to come back and fix that little problem with your friend . . . the Hollywood Ghost Club is always open."

"We'd love to come back," Luke gushed.

Caleb grinned. "Music to my ears."

I winced. I had an idea what was coming, but it was too late—I was powerless to stop it. Luke held out his hand to shake goodbye, and Caleb grabbed him by the wrist, pressing his own wrist to it. Then he did the same to Alex and Reggie while I watched, my stomach filling with lead. They each jumped a little bit when he made contact with them.

He pulled his hand back and the guys turned their

wrists over, seeing the initials HGC now seared into their shimmering skin. After a brief sizzle, the brands disappeared.

Caleb winked. "Just a little club stamp."

"Cool," Reggie said.

Caleb laughed—to me, it sounded straight-up sinister, like the laugh of a cartoon villain. The boys seemed to pick up on it, but they said goodbye after exchanging a glance. Although Alex's gaze seemed to linger a bit longer through the crowd. *Was he looking for me?* Once they were gone, I made my way over to Caleb.

"You never said you were gonna use your stamp," I said to him. "You know what that'll do to them." The guilt felt thick in the back of my throat—the anger, too.

He gave me a withering look. "Of course I do, William. But they're too powerful. I need them working for me."

His lips curled into another nasty grin. "And now, they'll have no choice."

21

Julie

Whoever said "better late than never" was obviously out of their mind.

I was so upset about the ghosts blowing me off, I didn't even want to look at them—much less deal with their useless pleas and apologies—when they came bursting into the school gym about three hours too late. Flynn was off raiding the cafeteria and vending machines to get some snacks for us, sustenance for while we cleaned up all Flynn's DJ equipment and the dance decorations.

"Julie! We're ready to rock . . . this dance, which is clearly over," Reggie said, bursting through the doors to the auditorium, out of breath.

(Which actually seemed weird, when I thought about it—did ghosts breathe?)

"We're so sorry we bailed on you!" Luke was right behind him.

"Yeah, the night got away from us," Alex added.

I looked at them, putting my hands on my hips. "Please tell me it had nothing to do with you getting back at Carrie's dad."

"Of course not," Luke said, while the others uttered their own protests.

Their reactions were too quick—it was shady. "Seriously?" I raised an eyebrow. "You're lying to me." Like ditching wasn't bad enough, now they had to add lying to it?

"It was something we had to do," Alex said, looking stressed. (Then again, when did Alex *not* look stressed?)

"But we'll make it up to you," Luke said, looking me in the eyes. "We'll play the next school—"

I cut him off. "What? Another dance where you can bail on me and make me look like a fool? Save it. You know what really sucks?" I met Luke's gaze. "Our songs are *good.*" Looking at the rest of the guys, I went on. "All three of you know what I've been through, and how hard it was for me to play music again. And then you do *this*?" I felt a pit in my stomach all over again, remembering what it felt like standing on that stage, looking out at that expectant crowd. "Bands don't do that to each other. *Friends* don't do that to each other." I swallowed. "This was a mistake."

Luke looked panicked. "You mean this dance, right?"

"No. I mean being in a band with you guys."

Just saying the words pricked at my heart and made my throat tighten. But I meant it. I had to mean it. It was the only way to keep from getting hurt again.

Before they could say anything else, I turned and fled.

———

I was still seething the next morning . . . so much that I missed my alarm and showed up late to school. When I finally got there, it was dance class, which was normally all girls. I tried to slip in unnoticed, but everyone was already step-ball-changing when I walked in.

"Nice of you to join us," Mrs. Kelly, the teacher, said as I slunk in. "Take your spot."

I slipped into the empty space next to Flynn. "Why didn't you wake me up?" I whispered, trying to fall into the rhythm of the routine as smoothly as I could.

"Because after the dance, you said you were never going to show your face at school again," she answered easily. "And I'm a very literal person."

"It's okay," I said. "It's those dumb ghosts I'm really mad at. I'd kill them if they weren't already dead."

"Don't blame yourself," Flynn said. "You can only be so strong when three cute ghosts ask you to join a band. And speaking of cute . . ." She elbowed me, indicating the classroom door and making me stumble at the barre.

"Right on time, Coach Barron," Mrs. Kelly was saying. And sure enough, behind Coach Barron was the entire lacrosse team, poised to partner up with me and the rest of my classmates. Which meant—Nick.

"You've gotta be kidding me. What are they doing here?" I asked Flynn.

As if she'd heard the question, Mrs. Kelly turned to face our class. "All right, students, Coach Barron and I have decided that his lacrosse team will be part of our class for a few weeks. Many pro athletes use dance to help with coordination and mobility."

Coach Barron nodded. "So this isn't about flirting with girls. It's about making you better so we can actually win a game." He glared at his players.

"Now, everybody pair up," Mrs. Kelly said, shooing us along.

Flynn was quickly whisked away. "Don't leave me!" I called after her, but it was too late.

"Hey." I recognized the soft, graveled tone of Nick's voice before I turned around. But then I *did* turn, and those eyes bore into my soul.

"Hey . . . you," I managed, just barely.

He opened his arms out, inviting me to be his dance partner. "What do you say?"

"Well . . . everyone else is already paired up, so it would be kinda awkward if I said no." *Also, I've loved you since we were in kindergarten and you cried when you couldn't get your glue stick uncapped.* "You think you're ready for this?"

"Sure." He grinned. "My little sister throws a lot of princess dance parties."

We started moving around the floor, tentative, but still graceful. "Not bad, Your Majesty," I said.

"Thanks." He paused, like he was deciding what to say next. "So," he started, careful, "last night's dance . . ."

Right. That. "Yeah. I'm hoping if I never talk about it, it'll be like it never happened. It's that whole tree-falling-in-the-forest thing."

"You'll be fine," Nick said, sounding way more sure of it than I could feel. "You're tough. You've been through way worse."

I was caught off guard, appreciating that he noticed what I was going through last year. I wouldn't have expected it.

Then Mrs. Kelly shouted a note to us, and in trying to correct our posture, we both tripped, until we were close enough to kiss each other.

If only . . .

We pulled apart, awkward. "Sorry," Nick said. "I'm just not used to dancing like this."

"Oh, come on—you and Carrie never dance together?" I didn't know why I said it. I guess some part of me just *had* to pick at the scab since things were feeling kinda, I don't know, personal.

"No." He looked away. "And we never will. We broke up."

My mouth dropped open, and I snapped it shut as quickly as I could. "You did?" I asked, trying to sound normal.

"I'm done with the drama. And I don't know if you know this, but she's not always the nicest person."

"I hadn't noticed," I said, rolling my eyes. We both laughed, and Nick stumbled again.

"You sure you want to be dance partners?"

"No—I want you," I blurted. Then I realized what I'd just said. "To be my dance partner, I mean. Here, let's start over. We'll get this."

Start over. It sounded nice. Nick was done with Carrie, which meant that he was maybe free for . . . other people? And I wanted nothing more than to put the humiliation with the Phantoms behind me.

Right now, dancing in Nick's arms, starting over sounded okay to me.

22

Luke

"Is this why we're here?" Alex asked. "To watch people take pictures of their food?"

I shrugged, just as confused as Alex was. So many things about the future made zero sense.

Alex, Reggie, and I were at some hipster café called Eats and Beats that was crazy crowded—mostly with, yes, trendy people taking pictures of their avocado toast. (And when did avocado become such a big thing?)

"It's fun," Reggie said with a shrug.

"Well, at least being a ghost has its privileges. I just wrote our names on the open mic playlist for tonight."

Alex snuck a glance at Reggie. "I'm worried about him. I think he forgot Julie quit the band."

I rolled my eyes. "And she's gonna come back as soon as she knows we got this great gig."

"But let's not forget, if she *doesn't* come back, we do have somewhere else we can play . . . and eat pizza," Reggie said.

Luke shook his head. "Dude, I know it was awesome to be seen by Lifers at Caleb's party, but we have that with *Julie*. We don't need him."

As if on cue, all three of us flickered, like a little jolt of electricity hit us, or we were a radio station that suddenly got tuned out.

"Ow!" Alex said. "That's the same thing that happened when Caleb stamped our wrists."

He was right—that feeling was just like the sizzle I felt when Caleb stamped us. I hadn't thought much about it last night. But the feeling was kinda hard to ignore right now.

"Feels like that time I was fixing my amp in the rain," Reggie said, and Alex and I nodded in agreement. It *hurt*. And it felt like it came out of nowhere.

Then again, the hurt wasn't much compared to how it felt knowing we'd let Julie down.

———

At least Julie wasn't hard to find. Actually, she found *us*, practicing in the studio.

And actually, what we were practicing was a special song, just for her.

As soon as she walked in, we belted it out, a capella.

We're sorry /
So sorry! /
We're super duper crazy stupid
SORRRYYYYYYY!

We all looked at Julie, waiting to see what she'd say.

"In case you missed it, we're really sorry," Reggie said.

"Yeah, I got that part," she replied. But her expression was hard to read.

"We've been waiting here for, like, three hours," Alex said.

"We almost sang the song to your brother," I added. "He comes out here a lot. Mainly to use the bathroom. Not our favorite part of the day." Then I got serious. "Julie, it wasn't okay that we flaked on the dance. We know we let you down."

"And none of us ever want to disappoint you," Alex put in. "You're the best thing that's happened to us since we became ghosts."

"So"—I jumped up and ran to grab the flyer I'd taken home from the coffee shop—"in the hopes you'll rejoin the band, we booked a new gig."

Julie took the flyer from me and scanned it. "So this means a lot to you, huh? Kind of like how playing in front of my whole school meant a lot to me?"

Reggie shot Alex and me a glance. "That sounds like sarcasm. I'm starting to think our plan isn't working."

I leveled with her. "Look, we know we messed up. But we need you in our band."

She narrowed her eyes at me. "Of course you do. Because no one can see you unless you're playing with me." Her voice lowered. "I thought the music we were writing together was special. But you're too obsessed with your past to even care."

And with that, she stormed out.

23

Julie

I won't pretend the guys' song didn't have an effect on me—I mean, I'm not made of stone. But that was the thing: starting to make music again, to write songs with Luke . . . It had opened something back up in me, made me feel things. So when they let me down, it hurt that much more.

Desperate for a distraction, I turned to my homework. But I hadn't done more than open my textbook when Alex and Reggie poofed in.

"Do you have a second?" Alex asked.

By way of response, I turned so I was fully giving them the literal cold shoulder.

"She can't see us anymore!" Reggie cried.

But Alex came and sat in front of me on my bed. "Julie, please."

I shook my head. "I told you, I'm done."

"We know," Alex assured me. "But before you decide forever, we wanted you to know—Luke is not as selfish as you think he is. Did he ever play you that song of his, 'Emily?'"

"No," I answered. "But I found it one day, flipping through his notebook, and he freaked out and grabbed it away. So I didn't ask any questions."

"Right. Well, will you let us show you who it's about?"

I had to admit, I was curious.

Slowly, I nodded, hoping I wouldn't regret it.

"Luke comes here a lot."

Alex pointed as we all looked through the kitchen window of a cozy, white-shingled house. An older woman placed two cups of coffee down on the table. She looked . . . well, heavy hearted was the only way to describe her expression.

"Emily's his mom?" I asked, trying to wrap my head around the scene.

"Yeah," Alex said. We watched Luke, unaware that we were outside, leaning against the kitchen wall, his gaze following his mother around the room. "He thinks we don't know, but we've been following him."

"All he does is hang out like this and watch them," Reggie said. "They never really do anything, though."

Now Luke's father came into the frame, equally weathered and beaten-down by time. Emily vanished from the window and then reappeared carrying a birthday cake.

"They're having cake. That's something," I said.

"It's a birthday cake," Reggie explained softly. "For Luke."

Tears sprang to my eyes, and through the window, I saw Luke well up, too. "I had no idea Luke was hurting this bad."

"It's even worse because when he died, he was on bad terms with his parents. They didn't want him in the band, so he just took off. And he never got a chance to make up with them."

Luke blew out the candles on the cake. His parents looked startled, but through the window, we could see them quickly write it off as wind.

"That's why Luke is so angry," Reggie said. "If Trevor had at least given Luke credit for writing all those songs, his parents would have known his dream was worth chasing."

I felt my heart crack in two. "They would have been so proud."

Alex looked me straight in the eyes. "We know how much it hurts when someone who should have had your back lets you down. We never meant to make you feel that way, too."

"Julie, we love our band. And so does Luke. Give us

another chance." Reggie's eyes were bright, filled with feeling.

I was filled with feeling, too. How could I possibly walk away from the Phantoms? They were my life now, my connection to music.

My mom was gone. And these guys—well, they may have been dead, but they were still here for me.

All that was left to do was to break the good news to Luke—and to wish him a happy birthday, too.

24

Julie

If I thought all my problems were solved now that the band and I were back together, I was in for a rude awakening. When I got home, I found Dad in the living room, sitting on the sofa with his arms crossed—clearly waiting for me and clearly unhappy about something.

"Care to tell me why you missed the first three periods today?"

Busted. "I overslept at Flynn's house after the dance. But there was nothing going on in those classes. It won't happen again, I promise."

Dad took a deep breath. "Okay. But if *I* know you missed class, it's only a matter of time before—"

He couldn't even finish his sentence before Aunt Victoria came bursting in. Her hair was frizzed out and her eyes looked panicked. "I came as fast as I could! Julie, I will not let you go straight into the gutter of life!"

"Tía, I'm fine. I just overslept. Dad and I talked about it."

She put her hands on her hips. "You are far from fine! I called your teacher and she said you missed a calculus test."

Now Dad stood, stern again. "'Nothing going on,' huh?"

Double-busted. "Dad, I'm so sorry."

"This is where you punish her," Tía said.

"I know." Dad sighed, resigned. "Julie, no more going out on school nights."

The open mic! I couldn't miss it! Especially not after having just patched things up with the guys. "But, Dad, tonight—"

"And go to your room." He cut me off. Aunt Victoria cleared her throat. "And study! Calculus. Go!"

I was still poring over my math book when the boys knocked on my door later that night.

"What are you doing? Just come in."

"We're being classy," Reggie said, hurt, as they came inside.

"Why are you still here? We go on in twenty minutes," Luke said. As if I needed a reminder.

I sighed. "I lied to my dad and now I'm trapped in my room all night." Even saying it made my stomach twist in knots.

"But we were just down at the venue and it's packed!" Alex protested. "VIPs, managers . . . it's kinda crazy."

I looked at them, desperate. We *had* to go. "What about my aunt? She's right downstairs."

Luke smiled. He pointed toward my bedroom window. "You're not taking the stairs."

***

I thought we'd be late, but it turned out we were too early. When we met up with Flynn at the Eats and Beats café, Carrie was just taking the mic. "Hope you all came here to have a good time!"

Alex wasn't lying—the place *was* packed. The tables were full, and it was barely standing room only.

"How'd *she* get on the list?" I moaned.

"Her daddy probably made a call," Flynn reasoned, eyeing my performance outfit with approval. "Pretty flowers."

"Dahlias, my mom's favorite."

Carrie's set was impressive, I had to admit. "She's actually pretty good," I said.

"Yeah," Flynn replied. "I kinda forgot why I hate her so much."

"Hi, girls," Carrie said, smirking at us as she came offstage. "If you're looking for Nick, he didn't come," she spat at me.

I smirked right back at her. "That's not why I'm here."

The MC took the stage. "Okay, looks like we're closing the night out with one more group." He peered at his list. "Uh, Julie and the . . . Phat Ones?"

Alex shot Luke a look. "Really?"

Luke shrugged. "I have lousy handwriting."

I rushed to grab the mic. "Yup, that's my band. Julie and the *Phantoms*." I took a deep breath and looked out at the audience.

From the wings, Flynn pointed at the "hologram machine" and flashed me a bright thumbs-up.

"Here's a song we've been working on," I said, a little tentative but getting more confident with every passing moment. "It's about the power of connecting through music. It's called 'Finally Free,' and I hope you like it."

I began to play, and the backup music swelled. *BOOM*. The boys exploded onstage and we went for it!

Hearts on fire / We're no liars /
So we say what we wanna say / I'm
awakened / No more faking / So we
push all our fears away

I got a spark in me / Hands up if
you can see / And you're a part of
me / Hands up if you're with me /
Now 'til eternity / Hands up if you
believe / Been so long and now
we're finally free

And I *felt* it, too—free and alive with the power of the music rushing through me, the energy of the crowd feeding us and our performance feeding them. *This* was what music was about—it was about feeling, believing, connecting.

I never wanted this moment to end.

When it did end, though, the night still had more amazing surprises in store for me. Flynn was waiting for me alongside a serious-looking woman who—I hoped?—was an industry person.

"She looks all business," Alex said to me.

"Who should do the talking?" Reggie asked. Alex, Luke, and I stared at him, waiting for him to realize. "Right, Julie should."

What with me being the only live, visible one and all.

The woman shook my hand. "I'm Andi Parker," she said. "I'm from Destiny Management. I'd love to talk to you about your—"

"Dad!" I blurted.

Andi looked confused for a moment, but then my dad stepped forward, a flyer in his hand and an angry glower on his face.

Behind me, the guys all gasped. We were so close! But Dad was clearly not gonna be swayed.

He looked at me. "Nos vamos ahora mismo. It's time to go."

The guys' second chance at stardom. My first. Maybe our *last*.

However you counted, it was all over now.

25

Julie

The car ride home had been quiet. Now, Dad and I sat side by side on the porch. All I could hear was the gentle chirp of crickets and Dad's breathing. I needed to apologize, but I knew that this time, it wouldn't be enough.

At last, Dad spoke. "We need to talk."

Yikes. That was ominous. *I might have preferred the silence.*

He cleared his throat before he continued. "After skipping class and missing a test, you decided to sneak out, even though I sent you to your room to study?"

Hearing him lay it out like that, it sounded even worse than it was. "I'm sorry."

"You keep saying that." He sighed. "And you didn't tell me you were in a band. If you'd just let me in, I could've been excited about tonight instead of having this conversation we both hate." He put a hand on my knee, imploring. "Why didn't you tell me?"

I swallowed. "It all happened so fast. The last couple of weeks have changed my life. When I play music . . . I feel like I'm closer to Mom."

Now he hugged me to him. "And I love that. But your aunt is right—school has to come first."

"I know," I agreed. "But the band's the only reason why I'm back in the music program. They played with me when I was trying to earn my spot back."

"They did?" Dad was surprised.

I nodded. "I think this is my thing, Dad."

He chewed on his lip for a second, mulling it over. "Look, I would be a jerk of a dad if I took that away from you," he said. "But if you're going to stay in that band, you need to keep up with school and keep me in the loop."

He was letting me stay in the band? "Really?!" I squealed, throwing my arms around him. "Thanks, Dad!"

"That woman at your show? I'm guessing she was like a manager or something," he said. "That could've been a big deal."

"Who knows?" I said, trying to downplay it. "Hopefully, she'll see us play again. Which I will tell you about."

"Yeah, you will," he said, standing up. "Because if I ever catch you sneaking out again, or your grades slip, I'm pulling the plug. Or whatever it is that makes those holograms work."

I stood up, too.

"Do I ever get to meet those guys?" he asked.

"Probably not. They don't actually live here. It's kind of hard to explain how it works."

He smiled. "You kids and your technology. Definitely beyond me."

I nodded. "Definitely beyond *something*."

Playing music again was a new thing. Telling Dad about it was another new thing.

And waking up the next morning to the smell of a hot breakfast: eggs, bacon, the works . . . That was *definitely* new.

"What's all this?" I asked, coming into the kitchen to find a feast laid out on the counter. Dad was humming the chorus to "Finally Free." I almost died from how cute it was.

"I was in the mood to cook breakfast," he said, sliding a plate to me. Sweet plantains! He really *had* gone all out. "After our talk last night, I felt like I might've cost you an opportunity with that manager. And I was thinking, I really want to support your band. So I called in some favors and booked you a local gig."

What? "¡¿Qué?! Where? Did you call your buddy at Drakes?" This was even better than sweet plantains, which was saying a lot.

"Not quite," he said, tossing a dishrag over one shoulder. "I called Flynn, and she said she'd help us throw a party here tonight."

I looked at him. "So you got us a gig at our house?"

He held up one hand. "Hear me out. You invite some friends over and play with your band, and I'll ask some colleagues to come over and film the whole thing. Give you something professional to post on YouTube."

Emotions swept over me. "You'd do that for me?"

He gave me a hug, smelling of coffee, bacon, and cinnamon. "¡Pues claro!"

Best. Dad. Ever.

I was grabbing some stuff from my locker that afternoon at school when Luke poofed in out of nowhere. "Ahh!" I shouted. Then I lowered my voice, trying to be discreet. "Normal people don't do that. Ghosts definitely shouldn't. What are you doing here?"

"We need to talk about what song to open with tonight," he said. "I think we go with 'Great.'"

"Hold on," I pulled out my phone.

"You're making a call? Rude," he said.

I ignored him. "Hi," I said into the phone, pointed. "Thanks for calling me. Otherwise, people might think I'm *talking to myself.*"

"Nice," he said, catching on.

"I think 'Great' is perfect," I said, answering his original question.

"Sweet," he said, pleased. We smiled at each other for a minute, until it started to feel a little awkward. "That was pretty much what I wanted to talk about."

"Oh, okay."

Then he took a breath. "I guess there was one more thing." Was I imagining it, or was a little bit of a blush coming into his cheeks? Was Luke . . . *nervous* about whatever this was that he wanted to talk about?

And was I . . . charmed by that?

"I just—I know I'm not the easiest guy to work with," he said. "But I wanted you to know . . . you make me a better writer."

A lump grew in my throat and for a minute I couldn't speak. Then I turned back to the phone. "I think we make each other better."

I felt a little charge build in the air. Was it possible to have . . . chemistry with a ghost? Because, if so, Luke and I were maybe having a moment.

I think he felt it, too. He looked at me. "You should ditch school so we can rehearse."

"I can't do that. I promised my dad school would come first. And anyway, I have to go dance with Nick"—*Right, Nick*—"who is headed this way. Okay, thanks for calling, bye!" I chirped awkwardly, putting my phone away.

Nick walked toward me, dressed for dance class. Beside me, Luke was giving him a bemused once-over. "Doesn't he look sharp?" he said, his eyes twinkling.

"Hey!" Nick said to me, oblivious to Luke (of course). "Ready for our big performance?"

"Oh, yeah. We got this." *Never mind how at our first practice we literally tripped over each other's feet.*

"Glad you're feeling confident. Even after all our practice, I think I'm actually getting worse. Good thing I've got a secret weapon." He elbowed me, teasing.

Luke leaned in. "Uh-oh, someone's got a crush on Julie," he sang. His lips were so close to my ear. *Ghost lips.* I had to remember that. And also, Nick. Beaming at me and calling me his secret weapon.

"Shut up," I said.

"No, seriously," Nick replied, thinking I was talking to him. "I'm nothing without you, Molina."

"You're great," I assured him. "See you in class?"

"I'll be the guy trying not to make us look stupid," he said.

Nick walked off, and Luke sidled back up to me. "Aw, he's cute," he said.

I grinned and flashed him a look. "Boundaries." He rolled his eyes. "I'll see you after school."

"Yes, you will. Now go kill it on the dance floor!" Luke busted a ridiculous move in the middle of the hallway. I was thankful, for once, that no one could see him. And that Luke didn't see *me* smiling as I walked away.

26

Flynn

"There you are," I said, finding Julie in the music room after searching for her everywhere. "Why'd you run out of dance class so fast?"

After tearing it up with Nick—seriously, their performance was *flawless*—Julie had raced off before the rest of us could even give her the standing O she deserved.

"I just needed some air," she said. She still looked a little flushed. "Things got kind of intense in there."

"Oh, I noticed. Dancing with a guy you've had a crush on forever will do that to a girl."

Julie shook her head. "The thing is? The whole time we were dancing . . ." She paused and took a deep breath. "I was thinking about Luke."

What? My eyes went wide. "Seriously? First off, I called it. Second, I know you always want what you can't have, but wanting Luke is next level." *As in,* afterlife *next level.*

"I know." She sighed. "And now I think Nick likes me. *Nick.*" For someone whose wildest dreams were coming true, she sounded pretty stressed about it.

"He totally does," I said. Maybe not helpful, but accurate.

"Ugh, this is so confusing. I like Nick—I have for a long time—but it feels different with Luke. We just *click.* He's so . . ." She drifted off, dreamy.

"Not real," I finished for her. It was time for some straight talk, before my girl got too carried away. "You can make all the music you want with Luke, but he'll always be a phantom.

"So here's what we're gonna do." I grabbed her phone and began to type. "Send Nick a nice little friendly text asking him to come to your party tonight." I showed her the message I'd composed.

"I don't usually send that many smiley faces," she protested.

"You do now," I assured her. "I'm not letting your heart get broken." Which it *definitely* would if she stayed hung up on a ghost. "Trust me—tonight, when you're playing with Luke? The key is avoiding those big, beautiful, *dead* eyes." I gave her a perky grin.

Julie looked at me. "You're awfully pushy today."

I decided to take it as a compliment. "You're welcome."

27

Alex

"Okay, let's try 'Great' from the top with the new harmony," Luke said. "Julie's taking the high part. It'll sound perfect once she's here."

The air in the studio was feeling a little stale—we'd been in there for hours working on this song—but Luke was right about how perfect it was, so I gave him a pass on the fact that we were way overdue for a break. And that he was way into Julie.

Of course that didn't stop Reggie from flashing me a little knowing smirk.

I gave a small nod back at him.

When I turned back to my drums, though, I saw it—a flicker of movement in the periphery. It was Willie, spying on us outside the garage.

"What's that about?" Reggie asked, nodding toward the window. Luke came up next to him with the same puzzled expression on his face. Spotting us spotting him, Willie darted off.

Oh, no, you don't. "I'm gonna find out." I poofed after him.

I appeared right in front of Willie, who swerved and skidded to a halt on his skateboard. "What's your problem?" I demanded. "Spying on me, and then bailing?"

He frowned. "I wish I could explain. But I can't."

There was an expression in his eyes I couldn't read at all. And to think I had felt like there had maybe been something between us.

"Not good enough," I said. "You've been MIA since we went to Caleb's club. I thought you and I were having fun together."

He looked truly distressed. "We never should have met."

Ouch. "Wow," I said quietly. "That hurts."

He looked at me, teary. "I'm sorry, Alex. I really am." And the thing was, he sounded like he meant it. Then he peered over his shoulder, like he was looking out for something—or someone.

"You're a great guy," he said sadly. "But I gotta go."

It was embarrassing, coming back to practice and telling the guys I had no idea why Willie was being so weird. But my embarrassment wasn't the issue.

The issue was that I'd actually started to have feelings for Willie. And I thought he had feelings for me, too. Was he playing me the whole time? And if so—why?

"You okay there, bud?" Luke's voice broke through my haze.

"Uh, yeah, why?" I asked, sheepish, like I hadn't been staring off into space for the last ten minutes when I was supposed to be drumming.

"I know it's tough, man," Reggie said, actually sounding sympathetic. "People say you don't forget your first ghost, and maybe that's true. But I'm sure there'll be others."

Who says that? It didn't matter; Reggie was just trying to make me feel better. "Thanks, Reg," I said.

Luke put his guitar down and perched on the edge of the couch to look at me. "You're a great guy, and a great drummer, Alex," he said. "Don't let that stuff get in the way of what you love."

"I don't know," Reggie mused. "Sometimes a little fire can make things better onstage. Like you and Julie," he said to Luke.

Luke looked taken aback. "What's *that* supposed to mean?"

Reggie laughed. "Everyone can see the way you look at her when you sing," he said. "You guys ooze chemistry."

I winced. "He should never say *ooze* again, but I agree."

"Come on," Luke protested. "I have chemistry with everyone when I sing."

Reggie and I shook our heads. It was different this time, even if Luke didn't want to admit it.

Even if we all knew that *that* relationship? Would be DOA.

28

Julie

"I can't say it enough, that was incredible," Flynn said. "And I'm not talking about my last slice of pizza."

The party and the show had gone off better than I could have ever imagined. Everyone we'd invited showed up—including Nick. We opened with "Great" and it was, well, *great,* just like Luke knew it would be. And my dad got to hear me perform with the guys. It was clear that he knew how important this was to me, now—and why. He understood that Julie and the Phantoms was special.

Now, Flynn, Dad, Carlos, and I were at the kitchen table, fighting over the last few slices of pepperoni pizza.

"So how do you do those holograms?" Carlos asked.

I faltered. I still hadn't come up with a good explanation for those.

Thankfully, Dad jumped in. "Don't try to understand it, Carlos. I don't."

"That's because you're old," Carlos said.

Dad glared at him, but it wasn't serious. "I'd send you to your room, but then who would do the dishes?"

I sighed, content, and took another bite of my pizza. My show had rocked, my crush (one of my crushes?) had come by, and things were great with Dad and me. I had my best friend by my side and my music again. This was the first time things had felt . . . well, maybe not "normal," since I was playing said music with a "hologram" band that was actually a group of ghosts. But . . . nice. Things felt nice, for the first time in a really long time.

I couldn't help but wonder how long that would last.

29

Alex

Maybe it wouldn't have been so bad that we couldn't eat the post-show pizza Julie was devouring if we couldn't *smell* it. But despite being ghosts, our sense of smell was still perfectly functioning. At least at Caleb's club, we could eat food, just like the living. After watching Flynn go in for her third slice of pepperoni, we had to poof out. It was that or die of deprivation. And we were already dead, so.

We hung in Julie's driveway. I found a basketball and tossed it against the hoop a few times. My heart wasn't in it. Honestly, it was all a little anticlimactic in the post-show adrenaline crash.

"Feels like we should be celebrating," Reggie said, reading my mind. "What do you guys want—"

That was as far as we got before we were hit with another of those insane flickers. "Ahh!" This one was way worse than last time. We all doubled over, grabbing our chests and moaning.

"Not that," I said, once we'd recovered. I still felt shock waves running through my body, like little electric aftershocks in my bones.

"I know they've been happening on and off all week. But that wasn't like the other ones," Luke said, stating aloud what we all already knew. He looked grim. "It's getting worse."

"Why is this happening to us?" Reggie groaned.

"Because you're in serious trouble."

It was a voice I recognized. A voice I knew and missed. One I'd once trusted. I turned. "Willie?"

He was somber. "We need to talk."

"So all these jolts we're feeling are because Caleb put his stamp on us?" Luke asked. We'd walked to the Orpheum while we paced and listened to what Willie had to say. And—boy—it was a lot.

"He's threatened by you," Willie said. "He needs you under his control. You're the only ghosts we know who can be visible to Lifers without his help."

I couldn't believe what I was hearing. I'd never felt so betrayed. "And you let him do this to us?" I asked, choking back a sob.

"I couldn't stop him," Willie said, looking racked with

guilt. "He owns my soul. He owns *everyone's* souls. If he knew I was here talking to you, he'd destroy me."

"So if we don't join his club, we'll keep having these weird power-outage things until we have no power left at all?"

Willie looked away. "Yes."

"And what exactly happens when our power goes out?" Reggie asked.

"That's it," Willie said, quiet. "You're done. You just don't exist anymore. Not anywhere."

We were silent for a moment, but then Luke broke the spell. "So we have no choice? We have to say goodbye to Julie and everything we've built together and work for Caleb?" He looked wrecked. I understood; I felt exactly the same way.

"You have another option. That's why I'm here," Willie said.

"Another *option*," I scoffed, so over Willie and his extreme betrayal.

"Please just hear me out. If you guys could figure out what your unfinished business is and do it in time, you could cross over and be free from Caleb and all of this."

Luke looked curious. "Okay. So what's our unfinished business?"

Willie looked stricken. "I don't know," he admitted. "But since you all died at the same time, it might be something you need to do together."

I glared at him. "Why should we believe anything you say?"

"Because . . ." He looked away, gathering himself. "Because I care about you, Alex. And I hate that I led you and your friends into this mess."

"Me too," I snapped.

"I can't be away much longer," he said. "I'm sorry. For everything."

I wanted to protest, but he vanished too quickly.

"This is all my fault," I said. "I met Willie, he led us to Caleb, and now we're screwed."

"Our dream is being ripped away from us again," Luke said.

"We need to tell Julie," Reggie said.

"We can't," Luke snapped. "This just means more loss in her life. But if we don't want Caleb to own our souls, we better figure out our unfinished business—fast."

My stomach sank. "Like that's gonna be so easy. There's so many things we wanted to do."

Luke pointed to the marquis we were standing beneath. "But the night we died, there was one thing we wanted to do. *Together.*"

Reggie looked disappointed as he put it together. "Play the Orpheum. But getting that gig was impossible. It took us years, calling in every favor we had."

Another power surge flickered through us, sending us to our knees on the street. When it passed, Luke looked at us, completely defeated.

"We don't have years."

30

Julie

At Los Feliz High, you know you've hit the big time when random students are coming up to you at your locker, asking to take a selfie with you. Which was happening to me more and more these days, especially since the party performance. I was just taking a request between classes, with some freshman I'd never said three words to, when Nick showed up, amused by my recent "fame."

"Can I get a selfie, too?" he teased.

"I'll have to check with my security," I joked.

"You laugh, but after your performance last night, it's pretty clear: You guys are going to blow up."

"It was just a garage party," I reminded him.

"An *awesome* garage party. Thanks for inviting me. So, listen, since we make such a great team—you know, with our dance and everything—and you're getting an A in history, any chance we could be study partners?"

This was surreal. I thought for a minute how many times I wished Nick would ask me this.

"I'd love to," I said gently. "But with the band, I'm not sure how much free time I'm going to have. Sorry."

He tried to shrug it off. "Naw, I get it. Then I'll ask you this: Do you think you could find enough time to go on a date?"

"Wow. Nick wants to go on a date with me." *Wait— had I said that out loud?*

I blushed. "Which, you know. Because you're him."

He laughed. "I am."

I thought about it, really *thought* about it, for a moment. Part of me had almost blurted out *yes* on pure impulse. But then, Luke's eyes flashed in my mind. It was all so confusing. No matter what my history was with Nick, this wasn't the right time for us to be anything more than friends.

"I am so flattered," I said. "I mean, you're great. Really great. But here's the thing."

"You like someone else, don't you?"

I sighed. "Yeah, kinda."

"Guess I missed my chance," he said, sounding disappointed but obviously trying to be cool about it. "Okay, then. Uh, still dance partners, though, right?"

That, I could do. "Of course."

I should have known Flynn was waiting in the wings, watching the whole exchange with Nick go down. As soon as he was out of earshot, she swooped in. "That was more than a 'what's up.'"

"He wanted to go on a date. And I said no."

She blinked. "What?"

"You said it yourself. This Luke thing isn't going away, so I figured, why waste Nick's time?"

Flynn's expression softened. "Aww, my baby's all grown up. She's choosing to like someone who doesn't really exist . . . But she's all grown up."

"But he *does* exist. To me. I know he's just air, or whatever. But we connect in so many other ways. The songs we write—we're drawing from the same pain. We both know how it feels to lose our moms." I paused. "It's just, he's hurting so much; I wish I could help him."

"Maybe you could write him a song that would make him feel better?"

I thought about that, then threw my arms around her.

"Flynn, you're a genius!" I moved to leave, but she called to me.

"You still have class!"

"Like I said," I repeated, changing course. "Genius!"

31

Julie

Here goes nothing.

I'd been standing on the doorstep of Luke's parents'
house for almost ten minutes, frozen in place. It was time
to make a move. I reached up to knock on the door—

Which was when Luke poofed in, right in front of me.

"What are you doing here?" He looked totally
shocked.

"Luke!" I was surprised, too, though maybe I shouldn't
have been. "Okay, I kind of wanted to know more about
you, you know, just curious. So I came here last week.
On your birthday."

His cheeks flushed with a combination of anger and
embarrassment. "What happened to all those speeches
about boundaries?"

"I'm sorry. But I've been worried about you." He

looked away, but I pushed forward. "I get it. It's hard when you want to talk to someone you love and you can't. I feel that way every day." Even talking about it now, I felt that dull ache in the center of my chest, thinking about Mom.

Luke sighed. "I wouldn't know what to say to her, even if I could."

"Yes, you do," I told him. "And you already said it."

"I don't understand."

You will. "Trust me?"

Luke took a beat, then reached out and rang the doorbell, pressing firmly so the chime echoed between us in the still air. I took a moment to appreciate how strong his ghost skills had grown since he first poofed into my life.

The door swung open and I was face-to-face with Luke's father. "Hi," I said. "My name is Julie, and I believe you had a son named Luke."

He squinted, like he was trying to place me from somewhere and coming up short. "That's right. Who are you again?"

"Julie Molina. Your son's band used to play in my family's garage." *Technically not a lie.* I pulled a piece of paper out of my backpack. "I came across one of his old songs, and I thought you might be interested."

Luke's mother appeared at the door. "Did I hear the bell?"

"This is Julie," his father said, a little hitch in his voice giving away some emotion. "She lives in a house where

Luke and the band used to rehearse. She was just telling me she found a song Luke wrote."

"It's about a girl named Emily," I said.

Luke's mom looked stunned. "I'm Emily."

I looked her in the eyes. "I think your son may have written this song for you."

I couldn't change Luke's past any more than I could change my own. No one could. But I could help him bring his mother some peace. And maybe himself, too.

32

Luke

I couldn't believe Julie helped me find exactly the right way to talk to my mom again. When she played them my song, I was able to tell my mom the things I never had the chance to say when I was alive.

And I couldn't believe I was going to have to leave her behind—again.

"I . . . I didn't mean to overstep," Julie said, after we'd left my parents. We were sitting on her porch, an awkward silence hanging in the air.

"No . . . that was . . ."

"You don't have to say anything."

"Yes, I do," I said. "I didn't really have any regrets in life, except for walking out on them. Especially my mom. What you did was perfect, thank you."

"You helped me feel more connected to my mom," Julie said. "I wanted to do the same for you."

I put my hand next to hers and imagined—just for a second—that they were actually touching. "This is an interesting little relationship you and I have."

She blushed, and I felt my own cheeks get hot when she smiled back at me.

"Oh my gosh!" Julie said, suddenly sitting up straight. "I forgot to tell you; Flynn said the video that my dad took of us playing the party is trending on YouTube!"

I couldn't look her in the eye. She was going to be so disappointed when she learned everything Willie had told us about Caleb.

"That's a good thing," she prodded. "It means people love our music. I guarantee you we'll get calls from managers now."

Time to face the music. Zero pun intended. I didn't know how I was going to say this . . . "There's something I need to tell you."

"Okay." Julie looked nervous.

"We figured out that we've got some unfinished business, and that's why we came back as ghosts. We have to play the show we never got to play."

"At the Orpheum? That makes sense."

"But we don't have a lot of time."

Julie's eyes widened in alarm. "Are you okay?"

"No," I told her. "We're in trouble. We made a mistake, did some stuff we shouldn't have. That night we missed the dance, we met a ghost who put some kind of curse on us. If we don't do what he says, he'll steal our souls, basically. Destroy us."

Concern flooded her face. "Then you gotta do what he says. What does he want?"

"He wants us to be in his house band for eternity. But if we can play the Orpheum soon, we'll avoid all that and cross over."

Realization dawned on Julie slowly. "'Cross over' as in what? Like, go to heaven?"

I crossed my fingers. "That's what we're banking on."

She shook her head, holding back tears. "That's just great."

She stood up and gave me a pleading look. I started to stand up and reach for her. But there was nothing I could say, nothing I could do, to make things better. So instead, I watched her go.

33

Julie

"You can't get rid of me. I'm like the Krazy Glue of best friends."

Flynn was organizing the trunk in my bedroom filled with my mother's stuff. I had told her everything about the guys crossing over, how they had no choice or they'd end up cursed for eternity. There wasn't much to say, so instead she was just here. That was enough.

"Right when my life's perfect. Awesome friend, awesome band, awesome guy . . . then bam!" I watched her fold up one of my mother's sweaters to put it in the trunk. "You don't have to do that."

She shrugged. "I know, but I get to check out all your mom's cool stuff." She gasped. "Whoa. Did you know this was in here?"

I looked—she was holding up a Sunset Curve T-shirt.

"What? The guys said they didn't know my mom. Why would they lie?"

"Maybe they didn't." A look of realization flitted across Flynn's face. "Maybe *she* knew *them*. She could have been a fan."

"Sunset Curve was playing the Hollywood club scene around then," I said, considering. My mom was a musician, and she'd been a regular at all the clubs. She loved watching the up-and-coming bands emerge. And that's exactly what Sunset Curve had been.

Flynn sat up straight. "Oh my gosh. What if you were right? What if the guys *are* connected to your mom? You know, through music or something?"

"Because she bought a T-shirt?" That felt like a stretch.

"Think about it—they were the ones who made you want to play music again. Maybe she knew they could help you!"

I didn't know how to process this. "So you're telling me she's out there somewhere planning all this? Why not just tell me to start singing again herself?"

"Maybe she can't," Flynn said. "Maybe she has to do it another way. Like by sending you signs. Think about it— we've been through these clothes how many times and didn't find this T-shirt until now. Why? This is another sign."

"*Really?* Signs?" Since when did we believe in signs?

"You're in a *ghost* band. It is a crazy world," she pointed out. "Look, you're gonna lose them no matter what. They helped bring *you* back to life; now it's your turn to help them. They have to cross over." She tilted her head. "Let them go."

I looked at the T-shirt, still in Flynn's hands. I'd only just found them—found my music again.

Could I let them go? Was I really ready?

———

I found the guys in the garage, moping. Alex was draped on the couch and Luke and Reggie were slumped against the wall, Luke staring glumly into space and Reggie strumming the same chord on his guitar over and over again.

"Snap out of it!" I shouted, sending Alex tumbling onto the floor.

"Jeez, you broke Alex," Reggie said as Alex got up and dusted himself off.

"Do you guys want to cross over or what?"

All three guys gave me dumbstruck expressions. "Get. It. Together," I said slowly, enunciating.

"But they're never gonna let us play the Orpheum," Luke said.

"This isn't over. There's a reason we were brought together. To help each other."

"It's like Luke said," Alex protested. "People don't just play the Orpheum because they want to."

I gave them a smile. "People don't," I agreed. "But *ghosts* do."

34

Alex

"How'd it go?"

Reggie, Luke, and I were sitting on a bench in front of the Orpheum, just looking at the marquis that *didn't* have our name on it. This was going to work, right? *It had to.*

"When that opening band wakes up, they're gonna find their bus two hundred miles outside Vegas with no chance of getting back on time." Willie smiled. He'd been happy to help when we explained the plan to him—to try to make up for what he'd done.

I put a hand on his shoulder. "I know what you're risking. Thank you."

"I'd do anything for you," he said.

I pulled him in for a quick hug. "You better get out of here before Caleb catches you with us."

He nodded. "I won't forget you," he said, before poofing out.

Me, either.

"You okay?" Reggie asked. I nodded.

"Thanks to Willie, Panic! At The Disco needs a new opening band. And someone up there needs to know we're available."

We were getting better at this ghost stuff. Our last poof had taken us right into the office of one angry club promoter, who was in the process of demanding to know how a tour bus drives itself into the desert. "Stop saying the bus drove itself!" he was shouting into his phone when we appeared.

His unlucky assistant (her nameplate said TASHA) sat at a smaller desk in his office, trembling as she listened to him shout into the phone. With my smoothest dance move, I knocked a cup of pens off her desk. And when she turned to pick them up off the floor, it was just a few taps of her keyboard to call up the YouTube clip of the Phantoms performing. Tasha straightened in her seat, blinking at the screen in confusion.

But after a minute, I watched her eyes widen. Confusion became excitement.

The clatter of the promoter slamming down his

handset filled the room. "Tasha!" he bellowed. "Get me CJ! Tell him I need a band to open in three hours!"

"Sure, Frank," Tasha said. She was already turning her laptop to face him. "But you might want to check this out first."

Reggie leaned against the wall, arms crossed over his chest, and flashed a knowing grin at Luke and me. *The plan was working!*

Tasha held her hands up like *I don't know.* "Somehow this video just started playing on my laptop. It's got half a million hits in just two days."

Frank actually moved to her to get a closer look. "Who are they?"

Tasha read from the description on the screen. "They're a hologram band. They call themselves"—she squinted—"Julie and the Phantoms."

"Tell your friends," Reggie whispered.

"Where are they located?"

She smiled. "That's the best part. Our very own city of angels."

Frank nodded, decisive. "Book 'em."

The guys and I cheered—then realized Tasha was looking for a way to get in touch with us. Quickly, I grabbed a pen and scribbled Julie's number on a Post-it.

Luke nodded. "Good thinking."

Good thinking? This was *great* thinking! The best idea

we'd had in our—well, did it count as our lives if our lives were technically over?

And it was all thanks to Julie.

<hr />

She was waiting for us in the studio when we poofed back. She looked nervous and excited at the same time—basically how we were feeling. She was pacing back and forth like one of those power walkers you used to see at the mall. (Where did they all *go* in the last twenty-five years? Was it just all SoulCycle and barre class now?)

She stopped in her tracks when we poofed in, talking a mile a minute. "Oh my gosh, what took you so long? How did Willie do? Did you get to the promoter? Did he see the video? Did he like us? Are we playing tonight? Why isn't anyone talking? Somebody say something!"

"You're not giving us a chance!" Luke said, laughing. "That's a lot of questions. But it's fine, everything's fine."

I nodded. "You should be getting a call right about . . . now." We all stared at Julie's phone.

Nothing.

I tried again. "Okay. Now."

Nope. This was getting awkward.

Finally, her phone rang, the shrill jangle sending us all a few inches into the air. We were jumpy!

Julie grabbed it. "Hello?"

She held it out so we could hear both sides of the conversation. "Hi, this is Tasha from the Orpheum in Hollywood. Is this Julie of Julie and the Phantoms?"

Julie did a little silent dance of excitement and then composed herself to reply. "Yes, it is."

And just like that, our plan was falling into place. Forget the jolts from Caleb—which, by the way, were getting more painful, and harder to ignore. The only electricity we'd be seeing tonight would be when we lit it up onstage—at *the Orpheum*!

35

Alex

"We need to go over our set list," Luke said, holding up his ever-present, battered notebook. "Julie was thinking we could open with 'Stand Tall.'"

"Sounds good," Reggie said, distractedly tuning his guitar while he sat on the couch. The mood had definitely shifted a little from when we first heard we were playing the Orpheum. As the hours passed, it started to dawn on us—if this worked, we were crossing over. As in: away from here, to some unknown otherwise. Suddenly, we were starting to wonder—were we making the right choice?

"*Sounds good?*" Luke gave him a look. "I wanna hear it sounds *awesome*. I know this isn't how we wanted things to turn out, but we're all in tonight. We're getting a second chance to play the *Orpheum*!" He was trying so hard to be a cheerleader; it was sweet.

"I get it," Reggie said. "But it's hard. Do we even know what's on the other side when we cross over? Do we still get to hang together?" He was trying to be cool, but I could hear the quiver in his voice. "You guys are the only family I have."

I felt a little stab of uncertainty in my own chest. "I don't know what's gonna happen. But it's not like we have a choice."

As if on cue, we were all suddenly racked by a searing jolt, so intense I felt it all the way down my spine. Reggie rubbed at his wrist. "Pretty sure we do. And it rhymes with Hollywood Ghost Club."

Julie rushed in carrying a garment bag, in frantic pre-gig mode. The door to the garage swung open behind her and stayed that way, but we were all too amped to notice or worry about being discreet just then. She immediately sensed our weird vibe. "What's wrong?"

"We just got rocked pretty hard by one of those jolt things," I explained, still feeling it in my molars.

"I think I ghost peed a little," Reggie confessed, and we all shot him a look.

"We're fine," I said quickly, mostly to put an end to any more talk about ghost pee.

"I was . . ." Julie kicked her toe along the floor of the studio, suddenly shy. "I was hoping you could do me a favor."

Luke looked up, serious and alert. "Anything, Julie. You know that."

"When you cross over, if you meet my mom, would you please tell her I love her? And thank her for all this?" Now Julie's voice was wavering, and I think there was something in all our eyes, too.

"I will," Luke promised.

He cleared his throat. "Okay, guys, band circle." We all formed a tight circle, Julie doing her best to rest her hands on ours. "I don't know what brought us here. But what I do know is, Julie, you're a star. And just because this is our last night together doesn't mean we won't be watching you from above. Now, let's give them a show they'll be talking about 'til the sun comes up. 'Legends' on three." He counted us down. "One, two, three . . ."

Together we all raised our hands. "Legends!"

From outside the garage, a horn honked. "My dad's taking me, so . . ." Julie gave us a last encouraging smile. "I'll see you guys there?"

Julie hurried out with her garment bag, and we thought that was that.

But we were wrong.

"It's going to be weird not coming back here," Luke said, looking around the studio a few minutes later.

"And where is it that you think you're going?"

We turned. It was Caleb, looming over us with a menacing gleam in his eye. We were all freaked, but Luke covered quickly, crossing his arms over his chest and going into defense.

"What do you want?"

"Such hostility. I'm just here to congratulate you on your big night," Caleb crooned. "Not everyone gets to play the Orpheum."

"Look, we know your stamp is hurting us, but like I said before, we already have a band. We're not interested in joining your club."

"And you can't make us . . . sir." I tried to sound as emphatic as Luke, but I kind of whiffed it with the "sir."

Caleb raised a sarcastic eyebrow. "Right, you're crossing over tonight. So exciting. Funny thing about the crossover. No one really knows what's waiting on the other side. But I know what's happening on *this* side."

Dread rushed over me. I wanted to reach out, to stop Caleb, but there was no preventing it. He snapped his fingers, and we were gone.

When we reappeared, we were backstage at the Hollywood Ghost Club, all decked out in vintage tuxedos. Caleb leered at us. "Don't you look nice?"

"How did he know our sizes?" I wondered out loud.

Luke elbowed me. "*That's* your question?"

"I know you boys aren't my biggest fans, and an eternity at my club might seem overwhelming. But humor me this one last pitch. For starters, isn't it nice that you're all here together?" He glanced at Reggie pointedly. "And believe me, everything you want"—this was for my benefit—"including Willie, is here. And on my stage, you don't vanish when the music stops. The connection you'll feel with the audience will be like no other." And that was for Luke.

From the orchestra pit, we heard the swells of an overture and the applause of the waiting crown.

"You hear that? Isn't it wonderful?"

A jolt sizzled through us, making me grab my wrist like it was on fire.

"Oooh," Caleb clucked, fake-sympathetic. "That one looked like it hurt. Let me remind you, you don't know if playing the Orpheum is your unfinished business. Do you have the time to make that mistake?"

We looked at each other, nervous.

"I suggest you accept my offer, because the clock is ticking."

36

Julie

My mom's trunk held so much more than just that one Sunset Curve T-shirt. I'd raided it for my shows and gigs since I first started performing again, and tonight I'd picked something special: her jacket, embroidered in bright stitching. I was admiring it in the mirror of the band room at the Orpheum—*the Orpheum!*—when there was a knock at the door.

It was Rob, the stage manager, escorting Flynn. "Hey, Julie, I've got your roadie."

Flynn gave me a little wink. "Holograms are good to go, boss."

I waved at her. "Best roadie ever."

Rob adjusted something in his headset, then turned back to me. "I'll be back in a few minutes to take you to the stage."

"Thanks," I said.

Flynn twirled a laminated card on a lanyard in my face. "See my backstage pass? I had sushi with Brendon Urie!"

"Good for you. I threw up in the car on the way over." My stomach was beginning to settle, but just barely.

"And you still look amazing," she reassured me. "Are the guys here?"

And there went my stomach again. "I haven't seen them."

"Maybe they changed their minds and took Caleb's offer?"

No way. "No, that's the last thing they wanted."

But wherever they were, I was worried.

A few minutes later, Rob rapped on the door. "It's time, Julie!"

"Thanks! Just a second!" I called out. I turned to Flynn, who looked just as panicked as I did. "Something's wrong. The guys were getting those jolts pretty bad as I was leaving. And there's no way they would stand me up again." I truly believed that.

Suddenly, it hit me. "They must have run out of time." A lump formed in my throat.

"I'm sorry, Jules," Flynn said, resting a gentle hand on my shoulder.

"They didn't cross over. They're gone. And I didn't even get to say goodbye." I couldn't bear it. I ran out of the band room, down the hall—past a very startled Rob—and right out the door.

When I got outside, I was in a back alley. Who knew Sunset Boulevard smelled like cat pee and old takeout containers? Not very glamorous, given that this was my Hollywood rock star dream.

What do I do? The guys were gone, but the saying was that the show must go on. Could I, though? Did I have it in me? First, I lost my mom. Then, I lost my band. Maybe today was the day I lost my music for good, too.

I needed a sign. I needed to talk to my mom. The fact that she wasn't here anymore didn't even matter.

I took a deep breath. "I don't know if you can hear me, Mom. But I can't handle this. Flynn thinks you're behind everything . . . I just don't know. If I was supposed to help the guys, I didn't. They're gone. I'm sorry. They were my friends, my band, they got me back onstage." A tear slid down my cheek and I swiped it away. "And I know it's where I belong, but . . . it just hurts so much. It all happened so fast. The same way it did with you." Now the tears came faster.

"I feel like my heart's been ripped out again. Yet here I am. The biggest club in Hollywood. And I'm even wearing your jacket. And maybe it is because of you, but I can't do this on my own. I can't. I just wish you were here."

That was the truth of it: raw and pure. I missed my mom. I needed a sign.

Just then, an elderly woman wandered past me, a bag of groceries in her arms. A bouquet of bright red dahlias peeped out of the bag. Without a word, she stopped and handed me one.

A shiver went through me. Those were my mom's favorite flower. That was my answer. *The show must go on.*

I ran back inside to where Flynn was desperately trying to reassure a very worried Rob. I held up the flower. "I'm back. I'm going on."

To Flynn I whispered, "Signs."

37

Julie

The houselights were so bright, I couldn't make out anyone in the audience. Which was a good thing, because if I had been able to see my dad, Tía, Carlos—not to mention, the sold-out crowd—I might not have been able to go through with this. As it was, my fingers were trembling as I sat down at the keyboard, laying my mom's dahlia on top of the piano.

The room was quiet. I cleared my throat and leaned into the microphone. "Hi. I'd like to dedicate this performance to my mom. She's with me every time I play. Thanks for not giving up on me, Mom.

"I'd also like to dedicate tonight to three special friends who brought music back into my life. It was their dream to play here. And this song is for anyone who's lost their way. Don't give up. Step into your greatness. Stand tall. And thank you."

Don't blink / No, I don't want to
miss it / One thing / And it's back to
the beginning / 'Cause everything is
rushing in fast / Keep going on, never
look back

This was it, my song, my moment, the music filling
me like air—like joy—and as much as I missed the guys,
in this moment, the music was everything. And it was
enough.

Whatever happens /
Even if I'm the last standing /
I'mma stand tall /
I'mma stand tall

And then—

With a flash of light, suddenly a drumbeat dropped.
Then my jaw did, along with everyone else's in the audience. It was the guys! They'd made it. They were here!
We were playing the Orpheum together! (And not for
nothing, but Luke looked *good* in a vintage tuxedo.)

We looked at one another and my heart swelled. This
moment was complete. We all felt it. We made one another
whole again.

Like I'm glowing in the dark /
I keep on going when it's all
falling apart / Yeah, I know with

all my heart / Ooh, ooh /
Never look back

But it wasn't falling apart, it was coming back together, at last. When the song ended, I turned to the guys. "I'm gonna miss you."

"Not as much as we're gonna miss you," Luke said.

We grabbed hands to take a bow, and the boys started to glow, brighter and brighter while the audience's cheers rose.

Then they were gone, at last.

Forever.

Everything coming together, everything falling apart.

38

Julie

There was a special kind of quiet to the garage when I wandered inside after the show. It was a different type of empty, knowing that the guys were gone for good. I wondered what it was like, where they were. If they felt happy, complete. Because that was how I was feeling after our amazing night— even though I'd always miss them, I'd never forget them.

I whispered into the air. "I know I said it before, but thanks, guys."

"You're welcome."

Reggie's voice echoed through the garage and made me jump.

"You guys are here?" I looked around and realized they were hiding in the shadows of the studio. "I thought . . ."

They flickered just then, Luke dropping to his knees.

"Oh no. I thought you crossed over. Why didn't you cross over?" And what did we do now? Judging from that last jolt, they were still getting worse.

"Playing the Orpheum must not have been our unfinished business," Alex said, rubbing his wrist and wincing.

"We wanted you to think we'd crossed over, so we pretended to. We just didn't know where else to go," Luke said.

"We thought you'd go straight to bed," Reggie said, looking disappointed that I hadn't.

"I knew you'd come out here, but no one listens to me," Alex said, miffed.

"Okay, you have to save yourselves," I said. "You have to go join Caleb's club *right now*. It's better than not existing at all. Get up. Poof out! Do something!" I couldn't bear the thought of losing them again, but watching them suffer was way worse.

"Sorry, not going back there," Reggie said. "No way."

"We got a taste of playing for Caleb, and it wasn't worth it," Alex said. "We couldn't stay there. We won't."

"The only music worth making is the music we made with you, Julie," Luke said. "No regrets."

My eyes filled with tears. "I love you guys." I moved to hug Luke. But when I did . . .

"How come I can feel you?" And I could—his body, sturdy and warm, pressed against mine.

"I don't know. I think I'm getting stronger. Guys!"

Reggie and Alex joined in the group hug. "Whoa," Reggie said. "I don't feel weak anymore!"

"Me, neither," Alex said. "Not that I was ever *that* weak."

We pulled apart, looking at one another in confusion. The boys reached for their wrists in unison. I watched in shock as Caleb's stamp glowed, then floated up off their skin, disintegrating in the air.

"What does that mean?" I asked, not daring to hope. "Are you real?"

"We were always *real*," Alex sniffed. "But now . . . maybe . . . we're *here*?"

"But, for how long?" Reggie asked, looking stunned. "Will we still be solid tomorrow? What about the day after that?"

Luke looked at us all, his eyes bright. "I mean, I *definitely* don't have the answers," he said, his voice hoarse. "But I think the band just got back together."

"Can we try that hug thing again?" Alex asked.

We did, and again, I could feel the guys' forms, their physical beings. It felt safe and true.

I had less idea than ever what was going on. I couldn't say if this was permanent. But for right now, that didn't matter. Sunset Curve was here. No—Julie and the Phantoms *were* back together, in person, unbelievably. Whatever came next, my bandmates—my *friends*—were here with me now, at last.

ABOUT THE AUTHOR

© JDZ Photography

Micol Ostow has written zillions of books for readers of all ages, including projects based on properties like *Buffy the Vampire Slayer, Charmed*, and, most recently, *Mean Girls: A Novel*. She also writes *Riverdale* novels for Scholastic, and graphic novels for Archie Comics. She lives in Brooklyn with her husband and two daughters, who would probably be thrilled to find a phantom boy band living in their house. Visit her online at micolostow.com.